The Secrets of
Grindlewood

ZORA'S REVENGE

The Secrets of
Grindlewood
ZORA'S REVENGE

JACKIE BURKE

LINDON BOOKS

First published by Lindon Books in 2016,
9 Raheen Park, Bray, Co. Wicklow.
Web: www.grindlewood.com
Email: jackieburke@grindlewood.com

Paperback	ISBN: 978 1 911013 46 4
eBook – mobi format	ISBN: 978 1 911013 47 1
eBook – ePub format	ISBN: 978 1 911013 48 8
CreateSpace edition	ISBN: 978 1 911013 49 5

Produced by Kazoo Independent Publishing Services
222 Beech Park, Lucan, Co. Dublin
www.kazoopublishing.com

Kazoo Independent Publishing Services is not the publisher of this work. All rights and responsibilities pertaining to this work remain with Lindon Books.

Kazoo offers independent authors a full range of publishing services.
For further details visit www.kazoopublishing.com

Cover design by Andrew Brown
Cover and internal illustrations © Fintan Taite 2016
Printed in the EU

About the Author

Jackie grew up with her sister and three brothers in Dublin. An avid reader and writer since her school days, she only recently began writing children's stories, having dreamed of doing so for quite some time. *Zora's Revenge* is the fourth book in the hugely popular *Secrets of Grindlewood* series.

Grindlewood is inspired by all that Jackie loves in nature: gardens, forests, wildlife, cats and dogs, and of course magic! Reading, hill walking and baking are just a few of her many hobbies. Jackie divides her time between writing and giving creative writing workshops to children and adults in schools and libraries around the country. She lives with her husband in Bray, County Wicklow. They share their home with a big fluffy cat called Millie.

Other books in The Secrets of Grindlewood series

The Secrets of Grindlewood (Book 1)

The Secret Scroll (Book 2)

The Queen's Quest (Book 3)

Othelia's Orb (Book 5)
Coming in Autumn 2017

'A classic tale to delight readers aged 8–12'
– Sue Leonard, author and journalist

Contents

Chapter One

ZORA RETURNS

Lord Vargon was excited at the thought of seeing his favourite student again. He had devoted many years to finding her, freeing her and bringing her home. Now her return was approaching fast. Audmund was patiently assisting the warlock lord, but he did not feel the same emotion. For months the old tutor and Wandelei traitor had worked side by side, but Vargon's fussing was finally getting on Audmund's nerves. Audmund had other things on his mind.

Zora's journey from the Outer Oblivion to Mord Manor had been a long one. Vargon had plotted her course, calling on sinister spirits to allow her safe passage from the furthest dimension, while Audmund spent his time concocting Recovery potions. Everything had to be precise or her return journey would fail.

Dark magic had banished her, locking her away in a bleak and lonely cube-prison for years. Even darker magic was about to bring her back and restore her to her former self.

Mord Manor was in a tiny dimension, created by Vargon after Zora's brother banished her. It was a large manor on a few acres of wasteland, surrounded by high walls and a dense forest, a place not on any normal map. After Worfeus got rid of his sister, it was unlikely the new Worfagon leader would show mercy to any of her allies. Vargon escaped capture and used his skills to create Mord Manor, hiding there while he carefully planned Zora's return. Later, he recruited Audmund to assist him as the big moment neared. The augurer had certain skills and information that were important for Vargon's plan to succeed.

Having pulled Audmund and Bodric out of their tussle in Bodric's Gorge, Vargon eventually agreed to let Audmund go back and rescue his injured dwarf-troll. The tutor had little interest in clumsy, muscle-headed beasts, but the big, bad-tempered pet might be useful later on. Until then, he would be chained up in the yard behind the manor.

Bodric Buzzard was excited at the thought of seeing

his old mistress again and he expected to be restored to a position of importance. Audmund ignored Bodric's boasting. He believed Zora had once used Bodric as a mere experiment to test her developing skills. But he didn't argue with the buzzard. 'Let him wallow in his fantasies,' he thought. 'Zora has a devilish side to her nature. All of us should be wary.'

Zora had been a strange child, fiercely competitive, vain and haughty. Choosing an ugly buzzard for a pet was unusual, though in keeping with her peculiar temperament. The sorceress bewitched him with the Mind-meld, a complex spell that allowed her to read the buzzard's mind and send him instructions whenever she wished. He had been useful to Zora before, spying on other children and even her parents and tutor. Her big mistake was not to also spy on her brother.

Vargon and Audmund were well versed in dark magic, but they needed an extra ingredient to complete Zora's return. That ingredient could only be found in the 'Verses of Doom', in the 'Chapter of the Dead', taken from *The Book of Darkness,* one of the four books that made up the WABOM – the *Wandeleis' Ancient Book of Magic.* The squirrel, Ripley, had located

The Book of Darkness in Hollow Hill, and no one had suspected him – not in time. He was quite happy to then switch sides when he saw an opportunity. Spying was a small price to pay if he was on the winning side, or so he thought.

Now the time had come: midnight on a moonless night at the end of winter. Ancient magical symbols were painted on the stone floor in the tower of the cold manor. The curved walls beneath the domed ceiling were covered with intricate images. Thick black candles sat in bubbling pools of wax at the centre of the symbols on the floor. Green and black smoke swirled from their wicks, wisping around the windowless tower, filling it with an eye-watering odour.

Vargon and Audmund stood in ceremonial robes: long, black, hooded cloaks, embroidered with silver threads and tied at the waist with wide red sashes. Ripley and Bodric had been ordered outside. They pressed their heads close to the heavy, studded door, listening, waiting, wondering. Bodric was excited; Ripley was somewhat uneasy.

First, there was a deathly silence, then a low hum as both men began to mumble. Their voices grew stronger. Vargon broke into a loud, piercing chant, while Audmund continued the slow, repetitive hum. It went on for hours. Wisps of smoke seeped out under the door and through the keyhole, forcing Bodric and Ripley to back away, their eyes stinging. The toxic smoke even singed their feathers and fur. Inside, Vargon's chanting became frantic, and then: CRACK! BANG! and again, CRACK! BANG! followed by several loud peals of thunder. A torrential burst of hail hammered loudly on the metal dome. Bolts of red and white lightning and further cracks of thunder surrounded Mord Manor. A violent whirlwind filled the tower, snuffing out all the candles. Vargon and Audmund stood in the pitch dark, pinned against the walls by the force of the wind. It suddenly became quiet, except for one loud thud.

After a minute or two, one of the candles flickered back to life. Through the grey-green, smoky haze they could see a crumpled figure on the floor. Vargon took a steaming goblet of red liquid from an alcove and approached the figure. She was in rags. Her long dark hair was a tangled mess covering her face. She grabbed the goblet and gulped down the potion, settling a little as it took effect.

'Welcome, Zora,' said Vargon.

The woman coughed but didn't look up or get up.

'Drink some more, my dear.' Vargon filled the goblet again. He gently pushed her hair from her face. 'See, Audmund,' he said, turning to the augurer. 'The colour is already returning to her cheeks.'

'At last,' said Zora, her voice cracking. 'I'm out of there. I'm back! What is this place?'

'Mord Manor, my dear, my humble home,' said Vargon. 'Let me help you.'

'I can stand by myself,' she said, pushing her tutor away and staggering to her feet.

There was little trace of the young girl Vargon once knew. She was taller than he remembered, and very thin. He could see fury and revenge burning in her eyes. She looked from Vargon to Audmund and then looked slowly around the tower, taking in the symbols, the candles, and the pitcher of potion. She gestured for some more. Vargon filled the goblet again.

'Audmund and I have prepared several potions to restore your energy and –'

'My powers,' said Zora. 'I want my powers. Audmund, is it? Make plenty of this stuff. I have much to do.' She gulped the potion so quickly some of it spilled down her neck. She tossed the goblet away and wiped her mouth with the back of her hand.

'Let me show you to your room,' said Vargon, and he led her slowly out of the tower. Ripley and Bodric ducked behind the door as it swung back with a deep groan. Both of them were quivering.

Chapter Two

THE FIRST MESSAGE

Jamie got up from the table and opened the door of the fairy house. Timber trotted in and sat down at his feet. Dougal darted in behind him, glad of a little shelter. It was sleeting again. He shook his coat, spraying the whole room, then sat down on a mat. Teddy had followed the children in earlier and was already curled up on Jemima's lap, purring.

'Why didn't you bring Trigger over today?' asked Jamie.

'He was helping Dad find a couple of missing sheep,' said Luke.

'I think Timber would like to see him,' said Jamie. Timber looked up and gave a little woof.

'Oh, this weather is horrible,' said Jemima, looking

out the window. 'At least when it snows we can take the dogs out with the sled.'

'Bad weather is often a bad omen,' said Abigail.

The others looked at her. She had a way of saying things that made you believe her.

Timber, too, sensed trouble was coming. He glanced over at Dougal, who groaned and put his paws over his nose.

Despite the wintry weather and the lack of news from Hollow Hill, the children had been busy. There was school of course, and Jamie had won his first fencing competition. Learning to fence had been fun, and all the practice he had had fighting magical enemies had given him quite an advantage. Both boys loved archery too and often spent time shooting arrows in the Grindles' big barn.

Reading was more exciting and more important than ever. Although they had been on two quests already, and seen and done so many extraordinary things, the children wanted to find out everything they could about magic, about Grindlewood, and anything else that might help on another quest. Abigail's granddad had given them lots of old books and they had already come in useful.

Abigail was still fascinated by her *Book of Enchantments,* though much of it was faded and difficult to read. Jamie loved *The History of Grindlewood,* a magical tome that updated itself. Jemima was working steadily through the twelve volumes of the *History of Magic* and Luke impressed everyone by solving all the puzzles in the *Crypto Riddles* book in no time at all.

They had been poring over their books when Abigail arrived a bit later than usual. Her teacher had encouraged her to enter a local art competition before the mid-term break, and she had just received word.

'First prize!' said Jemima.

'You deserve it,' said Jamie. 'It's fantastic.'

'Thanks,' said Abigail, blushing brightly as she opened out her painting.

'It's very good,' said Luke, 'but um, aren't they the Grindlewood butterflies, the ones we're meant to keep secret?'

'Very few people see them apart from us,' said Jamie.

'You're both right,' said Abigail. 'I did feel a bit guilty using them for the competition, but they're so pretty, and my art teacher thought they were so unusual!'

'Talking about butterflies,' said Jamie. 'I saw a new trio in the garden earlier.'

'Oh! If the new ones are here, something's definitely about to happen,' said Abigail. 'We'll probably get a message soon.'

'Yep,' said Jamie. 'Timber's very restless, the whole garden is.'

'I wonder what we'll be asked to do this time,' said Jemima.

Timber trotted over to the door and Jamie let him out. Dougal and Teddy hopped up and followed him outside. The malamute howled to call the rest of the animals and birds. They quickly gathered in the big kennel. It was big enough for most of them to squeeze into and shelter from the weather.

'Is there news?' asked Norville. The hedgehog nearly always arrived breathless and last.

'Jamie spotted new rainbow butterflies in the garden,' said Timber. 'Did anyone else see them?'

Surprisingly, no one had.

'Most of us have been staying out of this weather,' said Eldric. 'But we all know what new butterflies mean.'

'Messages,' said Dougal.

'Trouble,' said Norville.

'Another quest?' asked Ramona.

'Will there be a battle in the garden this time?' asked the old beagle.

'I hope not, Brigadier, but we must prepare for anything,' said Timber.

'I've been watching the sky when I'm out hunting,' said the snowy owl. 'It was streaked red after the last quest, but it's turning steadily redder.'

'Something must be wrong,' twittered the sparrows.

'I think it's a warning,' said Timber. 'We heard about the sorceress Zora some months ago, and we know that the traitor Audmund and that scoundrel Bodric Buzzard are working together. All of it points to trouble.'

'Don't forget all the stuff stolen from the Wandeleis,' said Eldric.

'Stolen by Audmund, thief *and* traitor,' added Norville.

'Why is that stolen key so important?' asked Cindy. 'You know, the gold one.'

'Everything that belongs to the Wandeleis is

important,' said Timber. 'It could be dangerous in the wrong hands.'

'You'd think the queen would tell us a bit more,' said Eldric.

'I'm not sure why she has been so quiet for so long,' said Timber. 'Something's not right.'

'Maybe she's busy,' said Teddy.

Suddenly, there was a lot of commotion. The children burst out of the fairy house, scrambling to get their coats on as they ran towards the kennel. They were following the rainbow butterflies who flew straight to Timber and landed on his head. The message wasn't that surprising:

We are Danni, Darlene and Drew,
We have an important message for you!
Come quickly now; no time to rest,
Queen Wanda wants you to start a new quest!

The butterflies flew from Timber to the children, landing on their heads to give them the message too. Everyone was keen to go right away, but Jamie and Jemima's father, Greg, came out of the house right at that moment and called them indoors.

'Now? Seriously?' said Jamie, under his breath. 'OK, Dad, coming!'

'What's this about?' asked Jemima, turning to her brother.

'I haven't a clue,' said Jamie. 'But I hope it won't take long.'

The children ran inside, followed closely by Timber, Dougal and Teddy. To their surprise, Luke's parents, Arthur and Alice, and Abigail's mum, Esther, were sitting at the kitchen table too. Trigger ran over to greet the dogs and Teddy. Jamie and Jemima's mum, Gloria, poured tea and coffee, and there was hot chocolate ready for the children.

'I was sorting through some old stuff in the cellar recently,' said Greg, 'when I found some papers belonging to my great-uncle George. I rang Mr Peabody – you remember, the solicitor who told us about this house – and he said he would like to see us right away.'

'Mr Peabody didn't want us to post the papers to him,' added Gloria.

'For some reason, he wants to see us in person,' said Greg.

'When are you going?' asked Jamie, thinking it

would be convenient if their parents were out of the way for a while, and hoping he and Jemima didn't have to go too.

'The day after tomorrow,' said Greg.

'Where's his office?' asked Jemima.

'In a small town called Butterville, about a hundred miles away,' said Greg. 'Mr Peabody said he might need us to stay around for a couple of days while he checks a few things out.'

'And Alice and I will be away too,' said Arthur. 'My cousin, Arnold, has invited us to a Finlay family gathering. Don't look so horrified, Luke – you won't have to meet all my boring old relations! Greg and Gloria said you could stay here.'

'Don't forget, you all have to go back to school in a few days,' said Alice.

'Cool, eh, OK,' said Luke, mightily relieved.

'I've organised some farm help,' said Arthur. 'So Trigger can stay here with you. The lads won't need him around the farm. We found all those lost sheep.' He petted Trigger on the head.

'So it's all sorted,' said Greg. 'Esther and Thaddeus have kindly offered to stay here and keep an eye on things – on all of you. They'll be in charge.'

'No pranks or mischief while we're away,' said Gloria, looking at her son.

'Huh, me, what?' said Jamie.

Arthur and Esther went home and Greg and Gloria went to check on their arrangements. The children finished their hot chocolate and ran back outside. They had to go to Hollow Hill and find out what was going on.

'That was lucky,' said Jamie. 'Our parents out of the way again.'

'Funny how that happens,' said Luke.

'My mum and Granddad will be here,' said Abigail.

'Sure,' said Jamie. 'But they know all about the quests.'

Chapter Three

THE NEXT QUEST

Jamie opened the trap door in the fairy house and they all climbed down, Timber too. They hurried along the tunnels to Hollow Hill. Professor Pendrick met them in the reception chamber and they followed him to the queen's outer chamber. Wearing an ankle length dress of dazzling blue silk and with the sparkling Tiara Lei in her shiny black hair, Queen Wanda looked beautiful. The children and Timber sat down in a corner of the chamber where there were comfortable cushions and chairs. The queen stood in front of the children and Timber sat at her feet.

'Last October, you recovered the WABOM, and my professors used its magic to free Queen Lyra from the Tree curse,' said Wanda. 'Then Queen Lyra chose to depart into the light and in exchange I was returned from the dead. We discovered that Audmund was a traitor and a thief, and the squirrel Ripley disappeared, probably to avoid being uncovered as another spy.' The children nodded. 'A lot happened in a short space of time, and we expect a lot more may happen very soon.'

'You mean Zora,' said Luke.

'Is she really back?' asked Jamie.

'Yes and no,' said Pendrick.

The children looked puzzled and Timber barked at the professor.

'My augurers have had visions of Zora, as have I,' said the queen. 'She is a dark sorceress, who was banished by her twin brother, Worfeus, a long time ago. He didn't want to share power with her, even though it was their father's dying wish.'

'She will come looking for revenge,' said Pendrick.

'But her brother is gone,' said Luke.

'Zora will still want to make up for all that she lost,' said Wanda. 'Power, wealth, control – and being a queen.'

'Revenge is in the Worfagons' blood,' explained Pendrick. 'And Zora had a fiery temper. I think we can expect a rather bad reaction to her long imprisonment.'

Timber stood up and spoke in witch language to the queen. He had been enchanted with this gift by the previous queen, Queen Lyra.

'Yes, Timber,' said Wanda. 'Zora is a grave threat to the Wandeleis. She detested us for being different, and – for other reasons too. I have spent the last few months finding out everything I can about her.'

'How is she coming back, and why now?' asked Jamie.

'We think someone has been carefully planning it,' said Pendrick. 'She could not do it alone.'

'The more visions we see and the redder the sky becomes, the sooner we expect her to arrive,' said Wanda.

'Where will she go?' asked Abigail.

'Somewhere secret, to allow her time to recover,' said Pendrick. 'The pages Audmund stole from *The Book of Potions and Spells* and *The Book of Darkness* contain the magic needed to bring her back and restore her, but they say nothing of where this should happen.'

'If you had visions too, Your Majesty,' said Jemima, 'does that mean you're an augurer now?'

'No one is permitted to take part in the augurers'

mystical practices,' explained the queen. 'But long ago, I developed the gift of *knowing* – a skill required before training as an augurer, and a skill that Abigail has. It seems to run in our family.' Abigail looked a little embarrassed. 'I gave up any thoughts of being an augurer when Queen Lyra asked me to concentrate on other magical skills instead.'

'What do we have to do?' asked Jamie.

'I have a number of tasks for you,' said the queen. 'First, I need you to recover the gold key.'

'It has to be *given* back to you, just like the WABOM,' said Luke.

'Precisely,' said Wanda.

'You should also know that our magic is still incomplete and quite unstable,' said Pendrick.

'But Queen Lyra did the Renewal charm,' said Jamie.

'Yes,' said Pendrick, 'but because some pages were still missing from the WABOM, our magic improved only temporarily. It has not been fully restored.'

'Many witches and wizards have trouble doing even basic spells,' said Wanda. 'Others cannot control their magic at all.' The queen sounded frustrated. She feared that their magic would not be strong enough to deal with a threat like Zora. 'I have all of Queen Lyra's diaries and personal parchments. Among them, I found a message about all of you. It was an old message I sent her before Worfeus caught up with me.'

'About us?' said Jamie.

'Yes,' said Wanda. 'I told her of my first vision of the *worthy*, those who would help us to right all the wrongs of our past – the four of you and Timber.'

'Wow!' whispered Jemima.

'Em, are there many wrongs that have to be fixed?' asked Luke.

'Good question,' whispered Jamie.

'The Ancients left us magic and a set of rules. One of those rules tells us how our mistakes must be put right – by the *worthy* – by you.'

Even though the children had heard some of this before, hearing it again was a bit spooky. They wondered what kind of mistakes had been made and what they would have to do to make things right again.

'I've had several visions of all of you,' said Wanda, 'including you, Timber.' She smiled at the dog. 'You are very important to us, and we will be forever in your debt.'

'Unfortunately, the Wandeleis have a murky past just as the Worfagons do, only different,' said Pendrick. 'We are two clans, but we are all descended from the same community of druids that once ruled these lands.'

'Since the time of Queen Cassandra,' continued Wanda, 'we lived in peace and harmony. The wars broke out when the Worfagons became jealous of our magic, and then we too made some terrible mistakes. Queen Lyra warned me that a grave threat was coming and I believe Zora is that threat.'

'*Grave* threat,' repeated Luke. He glanced at Jamie, who looked very cross.

'Are you saying that *we* have to deal with Zora, this incredible dark sorceress who will be really mad for revenge once she comes back here? And what has this got to do with Timber? He's *my* dog.'

'He is also one of the worthy,' said Wanda. 'But *I* will be the one to deal with Zora. Your next quest is to find and return the gold key.'

'Why is the gold key important?' asked Jamie, still feeling cross.

'That is one of our greatest secrets,' said Wanda, but she didn't explain further.

'Yes, ahem, we are working on a new compass brooch that will, hopefully, take you right to the key,' said Pendrick, glancing at the queen. 'It should be ready very soon.'

'That is all for today,' said Wanda. 'Lotus will bring you refreshments while I speak with Timber – alone.'

Timber stood up and followed the queen into her inner chamber.

Chapter Four

TROUBLE BEGINS

Timber and the children were quiet on their way home. Jamie was still cross. He wanted to know what the queen had said to his dog, but obviously it was another secret. As soon as they came up through the trap door into the fairy house, Timber ran outside to tell the other pets about the quest.

'If we need another magical compass,' said Eldric, 'then the gold key is probably somewhere not on any normal map.'

'Probably,' said Oberon, furrowing his brow feathers.

'The queen said Zora will be very dangerous,' said Timber. 'After all those years in prison, she will be desperate for revenge and determined to take back all she believes is rightfully hers.'

'How do we stop her?' asked Dougal.

'The queen is working on a plan,' said Timber. 'Our job is to find the gold key before Zora or her allies find it.'

'We know about Audmund and Bodric,' said Teddy. 'Who are the others?'

'Ripley might be involved,' said Timber. 'But the queen suspects someone very powerful is behind Zora's return.'

'Perhaps we should ask Gildevard to help,' said the owl.

'Why?' said Norville. 'We can't trust him.'

'That's not a bad idea, Oberon,' said Timber. 'And you're right too, Norville. It is hard to know what the eagle is up to, but he knows a lot about magical things and magical people.'

'Can we do something?' asked the sparrows.

'Your enchanted beaks are a great help,' said Timber. 'But I'm counting on you, the other birds, foxes and rabbits to protect the garden. The rest of us – dogs, cats and Oberon – will help the children to find the gold key and return it to the queen.'

'We've been watching out for Ripley like you suggested,' said Eldric, 'but we haven't seen him or Bodric.'

'Keep looking,' said Timber. 'That sneaky squirrel doesn't have any scent, so he will be hard to track down, and Bodric is always up to something.'

'How will we get word to Gildevard?' asked Teddy. 'We never know where he is or what he's up to.'

'I could check his cliff-top nest again,' said Oberon. 'But it would take a few days to get there and back.'

'No, we need you here,' said Timber. 'Don't worry about him. He's much too curious to stay away for too long.'

'Do you really think the garden might be in danger this time?' said Teddy.

'We'll be ready if it is,' said Timber. 'Ramona, make sure the rabbits are trained and ready. Divide them into groups and patrol the fields and forest. Eldric, alert all your fox buddies in the forest and organise patrols. Birds, spread out among the trees and keep watch. Make sure to get a message to Cyril and Serena over on Lindon Lake. The herons and swans need to be on the lookout too, and the ducks should probably move back there for a while.' Timber finished the meeting without mentioning his private conversation with the queen.

❧

An ice rink and fairground had been set up in a market town just six miles from Grindlewood village. Greg and Gloria decided to take Jamie and Jemima ice skating before they went to see Mr Peabody. The dogs would be going along too, as the family wanted to go for a walk around the stalls after the skating. But it didn't all turn out as they expected. Firstly, Luke and Abigail couldn't join them.

'Aw, Luke has to do a few jobs on the farm,' said Jamie.

'He must be helping his dad before they go away,' said Jemima. 'But I don't understand why Abigail can't come.'

'Her mum said someone called Elva was visiting to talk about her lessons,' said Gloria, popping her head around the door. 'Is Elva a new teacher at school?'

'Eh, I don't think so,' said Jemima. She looked anxiously at Jamie. The children knew Elva was Abigail's magic teacher.

'Maybe it's her, em, art teacher,' said Jamie. 'Abi's really good at art.'

A few minutes later, Jemima caught her brother in the hallway. 'Why didn't Abigail tell us about Elva? Do you think everything is OK?'

'I hope so,' said Jamie. 'She'd tell us if something was wrong, wouldn't she?'

Next morning, the family headed off early. Greg and Gloria watched from the side of the rink, holding Timber and Dougal on their leashes. Jamie was skating confidently around the edge, steadily building up speed. Jemima practised her spins in the centre until she finally managed a perfect pirouette. She was just into her second one when some unfortunate boy slipped, sprawled on the ice and crashed into her. Jemima was flung awkwardly off her feet and landed in a heap. She howled as she tried to get up. Timber lunged forward, breaking free of Greg's grip, the leash trailing after him. Gloria managed to hold on to Dougal, as Greg cautiously followed Timber over the ice.

Jamie heard his sister's cry and hurried over. He came to a sudden halt on the tips of his blades. Timber had reached Jemima first, having padded across the ice on his wide snow paws. He lay down beside her to keep her warm, and licked her face. It was clear that her left ankle was hurt.

When they finally got safely off the ice, Greg carried Jemima to the car and they headed off to the doctor's surgery in the village. The diagnosis wasn't bad; it was just a sprain, but the ankle was strapped up, and Jemima was told to rest and use crutches for a couple of weeks.

'This is awful timing,' said Gloria.

'I'll be fine, Mum,' said Jemima. She was more worried about recovering in time for the quest.

'With a few days' rest your ankle will be fine,' said Greg. 'Anyway, you can always read your books.'

'Um, sure,' said Jemima, surprised at her father's sudden cheerfulness.

'And write a few stories,' said Gloria, also cheering up. 'I loved the one you wrote about the trolls! Greg, did you know that Jemima is thinking of being an author, and Abigail might be an artist?'

'Trolls?' said Jamie, making a strange face at his sister.

'Remember Grizzle?' whispered Jemima.

Jamie nodded.

'Is that so?' said Greg. 'I look forward to reading a

story or two when we get back.'

'Thanks, Dad,' said Jemima. She had just noticed three rainbow butterflies fluttering inside the car, and pointed them out to her brother. That explained their parents' happy mood.

When they got home, Jemima was propped up on the camp bed her father set up in the study. It wasn't the most comfortable bed but at least she didn't have to struggle up and down the stairs on her crutches. Gloria brought down a collection of books, notepads and pens from her bedroom, but all Jemima could think about was being ready for the quest.

Jamie was just leaving the study when Gloria came in with a lunch tray. He had brought Ernie in to heal Jemima's ankle. The frog could heal injuries made by magic, and although this one was different, Jamie thought it was worth trying him out on the ankle anyway.

'Your lunch is on the kitchen table, Jamie,' said Gloria, entering the study. 'Here, Jemima, I brought my phone as well,' she said. 'I thought you might like to call Abigail and ask her to come over a bit earlier. I'll be busy this afternoon, as we're heading off in the morning. Are you sure you'll be OK?'

'Yes, Mum, everything's fine,' said Jemima.

Abigail's granddad answered the phone. 'Hello, Jemima, sorry to hear about the ankle,' said Thaddeus. 'How is it?'

'Not too bad, thank you,' said Jemima. 'Could I speak to Abigail please?'

'Yes, of course. Hold on, dear.'

In a moment Abigail came on the line. 'Hi, sorry to hear about your accident. Is your ankle very sore?'

'Hi, no, not too bad,' said Jemima. 'How did you all hear about it so fast?'

'The Wandeleis' grapevine,' said Abigail, 'otherwise known as Mrs Emerson. She's a very clever witch.'

'Wow! She really does know everything as soon as it happens,' said Jemima. 'Listen, I was wondering if you could come over a bit earlier. Mum said that Elva was calling to see you and I was dying to know what –'

'Sure. I'll come over as soon as I can. OK. Bye.' Abigail hung up.

Jemima put the phone down. Her friend hadn't sounded like her usual self: she wasn't available, she didn't want to talk, and Elva was visiting. What on earth was going on? Jemima picked at her lunch and

~ 40 ~

then started to read another book. Eventually she dozed off.

Teddy had curled up on her bed to keep her company, but both of them woke at the sound of the doorbell. Timber trotted in behind Abigail and sat down on the floor.

'Tell me what happened,' said Jemima eagerly. 'What did Elva say?'

'Sorry,' said Abigail. 'Elva arrived just when I picked up the phone. I was afraid I was in trouble, so I had to go quickly.'

'Are you?'

'Not exactly,' said Abigail. She made a strange face. 'I am in a bit of bother, though.'

'Oh? Tell me,' said Jemima.

'After I won the art competition, Mum said she thought I should join the arts, crafts and restoration class in Hollow Hill. She said I could learn how to restore *The Book of Enchantments*.'

'That would be brilliant!' said Jemima.

'I know. I'd love to do it,' said Abigail. 'But I want to learn spells as well, advanced spells, the kind we'll need on the quests.'

'Can't you do both?' asked Jemima.

'There wouldn't be enough time,' said Abigail, 'not with normal school as well.'

'I suppose,' said Jemima. 'Uh, oh, is there something else?'

'Granddad thinks I could be an augurer,' said Abigail. 'He wants me to really think about it.'

'Well, you often say weird things that turn out to be right,' said Jemima. 'Is that the same thing?'

'Sort of,' said Abigail.

'So you're good at lots of things,' said Jemima. 'What do *you* like best?'

'That's the problem,' said Abigail. 'I'm not sure.'

'When do you have to decide?'

'Very soon,' said Abigail. She sighed and shrugged her shoulders. It was too much to think about with a quest on the way. 'Tell me about the ice rink.'

Timber had been listening to the girls, but he was also thinking about other things. Every few minutes he stood up and walked around, then sat down by the door, under the window or beside the bed. Queen Wanda's words were buzzing in his head. Was he really that important to the magical people? He belonged to Jamie and the Grindles – he was *their* dog, *their* protector. How could he be anything else? The big dog put his head on his paws and groaned. The queen had said he must keep it secret for the moment, but he knew Teddy was bound to suspect something.

He was right.

Chapter Five

SECRETS AND LIES

Oberon went hunting as soon as it was dark. He didn't have much luck. 'Everything is still hibernating,' he thought. 'What a dreadfully long winter.' He flew on to the darkest part of the forest hoping to find a lone mouse or rat. But not this night. Then he realised he was very close to Worfeus' old lair. He flew on a bit and landed on the edge of the enormous cauldron. It was still covered with moss and ivy, but there was nothing in it except bits of old bones. Beside it was the small cave where Worfeus had once slept when he was trapped in the forest as a wolf. Oberon peered through the ivy that hung over the entrance and decided to take a closer look. He poked around for a bit until he spotted a lump of granite jutting out at the back of the cave. His investigations were interrupted by the sound of fluttering outside.

'Gildevard!'

'Oberon!'

'What are you doing here?' asked the owl.

'I could ask you the same question!' said the eagle.

'I was hoping to find some supper,' said the owl. 'Hunting has been poor lately.'

'Anything tasty in the cave?' asked the eagle, narrowing his eyes.

'No,' said the owl, glaring back at him.

'How is everyone in the garden?'

'Fine, thank you. Jemima sprained her ankle, but it's nothing serious.'

'Any more whisperings of Zora?' asked the eagle.

'We're still waiting to hear something definite,' said Oberon. 'Did *you* hear anything?'

'Nothing of interest,' said the eagle. 'But with red skies at night and winter storms continuing, there's bound to be trouble on the way.'

There was a rustle in a nearby bush, then quiet, then more rustling.

'Ah,' said the owl. 'Some supper!'

'Perhaps not,' said the eagle.

With that, a small blur of fur scurried out of sight.

There was a squawk followed by a muffled pop.

'Wait a minute, was that who I think it was?' asked the owl.

'Who do you think it was?'

'Stop playing games,' said Oberon. 'That fur could have been Ripley and that squawk sounded like Bodric. Are you in cahoots with those troublemakers again?'

'I'm simply hunting, same as you,' said the eagle.

'Hunting for what?' said Oberon.

'Why don't we try and catch something together?' said Gildevard.

'No,' said Oberon. 'Let's go and see Timber first.'

As they took off, the eagle glanced back at Worfeus' lair. He could always come back another time and check it out for himself.

Timber and Dougal had just finished their evening patrol when Oberon and Gildevard landed on the lawn. The animals gathered.

'We thought you might drop by,' said Timber.

'I found him in the forest,' said Oberon. 'Hunting.'

'We both were,' said Gildevard, giving the owl a

sharp look. 'Hello, Timber, everyone. You look ready for another quest.'

'Who told you?' asked Dougal.

'I hear things,' said Gildevard.

'Sorry I'm late,' said Eldric. 'It took ages to find something to eat. Oh, Gildevard.'

The eagle didn't reply. He didn't like foxes.

'We have been asked to find the gold key,' said Timber, 'before Zora returns.'

'Sounds tricky,' said the eagle. 'Do you know where it is?'

'Everyone knows that Audmund took it,' said Timber, 'but his whereabouts are still a mystery.'

'I'm sure another compass will help,' said Gildevard.

The animals shuffled. It made them uncomfortable to hear how much the eagle already knew, or guessed.

'So, Gildevard, have you come to help or just to say hello?' asked Timber.

'Why, both, of course,' said the eagle. 'I've said my hello now, so let's chat after supper about how I might help.' The eagle flew off. Timber nodded to Oberon and the owl flew after him.

Early the next morning, Greg and Gloria headed off to visit Mr Peabody. Thaddeus had already left for Hollow Hill, and Esther was cooking pancakes for breakfast. Jamie went to feed the dogs, but Timber was still in the kennel. When Jamie found him, he realised quickly what had kept him – the butterflies. When they were finished delivering their latest message, Jamie and Timber hurried back to the house. The others were anxious to hear the news, but judging by Jamie's face and Timber's growling, they knew it wasn't good. Jamie scribbled it down so he would remember it.

> *The Ancients knew a time would come when evil would abound,*
> *They placed the saving of their land in a brave and loyal hound.*
> *Through all of time, this special dog would guard, protect and may,*
> *In time to come, return again and fight another day.*

'It doesn't sound like the earlier messages at all,' said Luke.

'I don't like the mention of a special dog again,' said Jamie. Timber nuzzled his nose into Jamie's hand.

'Maybe it's not about Timber,' said Jemima.

'I think it probably is,' said Abigail.

The children spent a long, frustrating day wondering about the message, looking up their books hoping to find something that would make sense of it. There was no mention of dogs in any book that wasn't in witch language, and they couldn't read witch language, so that didn't help. It was infuriating. Waiting for the compass brooch to be ready was also getting on their nerves.

Thaddeus came in later and Esther gave him the news about the butterflies. 'Jamie doesn't like all the attention Timber's getting.'

'I don't blame him, but it may get worse,' said Thaddeus. 'He is such a special dog, and not just to Jamie, not any more.'

'Does Wanda really think it's him, the dog in the prophecy?' asked Esther. Thaddeus gave her a disappointed look, but didn't answer. 'She won't tell me even though I'm her sister. Can't you tell me, Thaddeus?'

'As the queen's adviser and professor, you know

I'm not allowed to say anything,' said Thaddeus. 'It puts this family in quite a pickle, all of us being so closely involved yet not able to talk about it, not all of it, anyway.'

'Well, tell me what you can, as soon as you can,' said Esther.

Thaddeus smiled, showing his mesmerising gold tooth. Esther scowled and looked away before it could take effect.

The next morning, there were more questions out in the garden.

'I've been thinking about it all night,' said Teddy crossly. 'What kind of a message was that anyway?'

The owl and the eagle flew down to join them.

'I agree with Luke,' said Trigger. 'It didn't sound like the other messages.'

'It could be about you, Timber,' said Dougal.

'Who else could it be about?' asked Eldric.

'Indeed,' muttered the eagle.

Everyone wanted to know what Timber thought.

'I think we should concentrate on our next task –

the gold key – and be ready when we're called,' said the dog. 'Everyone back to their posts, please.'

'I think there's something you're not telling me,' said Teddy, when they were alone. 'What do you think the message really means?'

'I'm not meant to say,' said Timber. 'And I'm not even sure.'

Teddy looked confused. They trotted towards the house and sat down on the patio under the kitchen window, away from everyone.

'Please keep this to yourself,' said Timber. 'I don't want to alarm the others.'

Teddy nodded and leaned closer.

'The queen told me that the Wandeleis used to have a snow dog to protect them. Tyrus was his name. He was their *guardian*.'

'I remember that name,' said Teddy. 'Queen Lyra called you Tyrus a couple of times, by mistake. And you are the bravest dog in the world.' He purred at his friend.

'Teddy, they really think I am descended from Tyrus,' said Timber.

'But how?' said Teddy. 'He lived too long ago, and anyway, you and I were born in Alaska.'

'That's true,' said Timber, 'but the Wandeleis believe I am their new protector, chosen by the Ancients.'

'The Ancients?' said Teddy. 'You mean, part of a prophecy from long ago?'

'That's what the queen said, but I didn't tell you that.'

'I understand,' said Teddy. 'It's a secret.'

'The queen said I would know what to do when the time comes,' said Timber, 'but I have no idea what I'm supposed to do or when, other than follow her instructions, and I really don't want to let anyone down.'

'You won't, you couldn't,' said Teddy. 'Like she said, you'll know when the time comes. You always do.'

Up on the roof, hidden behind the chimney stack, Gildevard had been listening carefully.

Wanda often worked late into the night. In fact, since she had become queen she had slept very little. Queen Lyra had left chests filled with scrolls, all with detailed instructions – and secrets.

She put her quill and ink away and stared at the pieces of parchment strewn across her desk. There was a pile on the floor too. They were scraps mostly, covered with inky scrawl that she had finally deciphered and transcribed onto new scrolls of parchment. When she was finished each one, she placed it carefully inside a safe that was built into the wall of her private chamber. With a wave of her wand, the safe was locked and undetectable.

Wanda returned to her desk. She had to finish the puzzle that Queen Lyra had started, reveal the map hidden inside, and find the orb before anyone else did. She knew the Worfagons would seek it out once Zora returned, if they hadn't been trying already. After all, it had once been in the Worfagons' possession, and stealing it had triggered the start of the wars. Both clans desired it, thinking it would make them more powerful than the other. But as time passed and the goblin thieves had disappeared, no one was left who knew where it had been hidden.

Both the Worfagons and the Wandeleis were guilty of many mistakes, grave mistakes, but Wanda was determined to put things right. Finding the orb was part of that goal, but until everything was ready – their magic restored and their possessions returned – she could only entrust the puzzle to a chosen few. It had been a heavy burden to bear.

The puzzle had turned out to be an enormous task and an enormous secret. Now it was clear to Wanda that she was going to need help, especially if it were to be solved in time. She had some very difficult decisions to make.

Chapter Six

PLOTTING AND SCHEMING

Audmund quickly tired of Vargon's fussing over Zora and updating her on the last twenty years. He made his excuses and left the room. Wrapping up tightly in his grey-hooded cloak, he headed out the back.

'Try to be patient, Grizzle,' he said to his pet beast. 'I have a cunning plan in play. We won't be stuck here forever with that arrogant lord and pampered sorceress.' Grizzle gurgled back at him, drooling and dopey from a potion Vargon had insisted was added to his food. 'Something to keep him quiet,' his lordship had said. Audmund wondered if that was all it was.

He passed through a rusty gate in the yard and around the outside of the manor's high perimeter wall. Soon he reached five stone pillars at the edge of a dense forest that surrounded the manor and marked the edge of the dimension. He bent down and placed each finger of his right hand on five small symbols carved into the side of the widest pillar, the Prime, and waited. A shimmering globe of light appeared in the centre of the pillars. Once it settled to a steady glow, Audmund stepped into it. The glow faded and he was gone.

Shunting from one dimension to another took its toll, particularly as Audmund had very little Worfagon blood in his veins – just a tiny bit from his great-grandmother – a secret he had kept so well that he couldn't understand how Vargon had uncovered it. It had been just enough to convince the wily augurer to switch sides.

He felt rather ill as he arrived through the smallest of portals, one normally only used by Bodric or Ripley. As he tried to steady himself, he had to swallow several times to avoid being sick. It wouldn't do to leave any evidence of his visit. He squelched through the mud in the thickest part of Grindlewood Forest and continued walking until he reached a well-disguised tunnel to Hollow Hill. It was narrow and steep. Sliding into the tunnel's half-open mouth, he pushed back the brambles and nettles that were trying to cover it. Once inside, he was forced to crouch for a while. After a few minutes of walking in a bent position, the tunnel gradually became higher and he was able to stand up. It remained narrow and claustrophobic, but he quickened his pace, shuffling along until he reached a small oak door.

A key was peeking out from under the door frame. 'Good,' he thought, 'my Obedience spell has lasted well.' He took the key and opened the door. Moving very slowly, he slipped around the door, aware that it was warped and might creak. He closed it carefully behind him and put the key in his pocket.

Hurrying along the dark, damp tunnel, he used the tip of his wand to light the way. He came to a bigger door with large iron hinges. This time the key and a little note were left in a crack in the wall. 'Better,' he thought and checked the note. 'An unusual combination of charms, but I think I can handle it.'

He opened the door, heard the subtle sizzle of the Protection charm, and instantly disarmed it. Continuing down the tunnel, he deftly disarmed the next charm and the next. A shadow emerged from around a bend and out of a tunnel that led up to the wizards' quarters. Audmund sneered at the thought of his former colleagues. 'That clever sleeping draught from *The Book of Potions and Spells* will have taken care of them for tonight.' He looked at his unfortunate accomplice who emerged from the darkness, completely entranced, unaware of what he was doing and possibly even who he was.

'Well done, Phineas, excellent work,' whispered Audmund. 'Now, to the vault.'

Audmund arrived back in Mord Manor to find Vargon in his laboratory concocting another poison from spider venom – his favourite pastime. The lab always made Audmund shudder, despite the fact that he was a potions expert himself. There were dozens of spiders of all shapes and sizes locked in glass cages. Some of them were hairy and twitchy and unnervingly quick. Audmund wondered how often and how many of them had escaped.

'Where have you been?' demanded Vargon. 'I wanted you to assist me with this experiment.'

Audmund explained, but he didn't get the reaction he expected. 'I thought you'd be pleased, My Lord,' he said. 'Now we have the silver key as well. Surely two keys are better than one?'

'I told you that four keys were needed to reach the orb because I thought you were intelligent, not so you could show off!' roared Vargon. 'You weren't supposed to steal any of them until I said so. Zora is not ready to fight the Wandeleis yet, and have no doubt, Audmund, there will be a firece battle when someone finally recovers that orb. Now please remember who's in charge here – I am!'

'Yes, My Lord,' muttered the augurer leaning back to avoid the large spider that Vargon was waving around in his gloved hand.

'Leave the silver key beside the tarantula cage.'

Audmund left the key as instructed and turned to leave, but his way was blocked. Zora was standing in the doorway.

'Did you say "in charge"?' said Zora. 'I am in charge now.'

'You should be resting,' said Vargon.

'No, I should not! And do not call me Zora. From now on I am the Red Queen, "Your Royal Redness" to all of you. Red is my favourite colour, after all, and only ordinary queens are called Majesty.'

Vargon looked surprised. Audmund did not. His

opinion was not clouded by tutoring the young sorceress, and pandering to the whims of the old king and queen. Audmund had met Zora a long time ago and thought her a spoiled and wicked child. Unlike her talented but buffoonish twin brother, who could be fooled if flattered or bribed, Zora was never one to be persuaded or controlled, and her demands were often peculiar and dark. Clearly that part of her hadn't changed, though Vargon might take a little longer to realise it.

'I always liked dabbling in poison,' said Zora, as she passed the rows of spiders. They cowered from her, all except the very biggest and the most poisonous ones. She stopped in front of a gilted mirror that stood in a corner of the room. It was dusty, hardly ever used. Gazing into it, she turned from side to side, considering her appearance. She smoothed her hair. It was dark, but streaked blood red, revealing how much red potion she had already drunk. Strangely, it was almost a perfect match for her long red gown. Her shiny new boots were black with red laces and they narrowed to a frightening point at the toe.

'These clothes won't do,' she said. 'I want luxurous gowns, the sort a *queen* would wear, *a red queen*.' She glared at Vargon, then at Audmund. Her voice rose as she listed further demands while she paced up and down. 'I want nice things around me, grand things, pretty things, delicious food, fabulous jewels, glorious gowns, gold and finery, and everyone doing exactly – what – I – tell – them.' She finished with a roar and a blazing stare.

Neither of the men moved. Already, Zora was extremely unnerving.

'So,' she continued, 'Grindlewood has a new army of children and their pets. Hilarious!' She laughed and then turned nasty again. 'They won't stop me getting what I want!'

'And that would be precisely what, my dear?' asked Vargon.

'TOTAL REVENGE!' she roared. More of her hair turned red and some of it frizzed as if electrified. Everything she touched showed a tinge or a streak of red, and it pleased her because she knew it irked the others. 'First, I will prove I am better than that silly Forest Queen. I will destroy her and her palace, and anyone and anything that gets in my way. I will take back what is mine and I will rule this kingdom with an iron fist. I will expand it beyond Grindlewood and make it the greatest kingdom ever known. I will hunt down and find all *our* lost treasures and make sure those little Wandeleis never lay hands on them again!'

Vargon looked pleased. 'That won't be too difficult,' he said. 'The Forest Queen doesn't really have a palace any more, thanks to your brother. And she still likes to live peacefully.'

'Whatever she has, I will take it or destroy it!' Zora roared. 'I am the rightful ruler of this kingdom. And I'm changing its name to Worfagonia, in memory of my father, Worfagus, the king who wished me to rule after him, and the Worfagon clan who will be loyal only to me or die!'

'As for taking back what belongs to us, I mean, to you, we have so much to discuss, my dear,' said Vargon. 'Let us retire to the parlour, and we shall plan your revenge and your triumphant return to – Worfagonia.'

'Perhaps you should start with the new Grindlewood Army,' said Audmund. 'They outwitted and defeated your brother, Worfeus.'

Vargon glowered at him.

'Ha!' cried Zora. 'Beaten by a group of children, their pets and those butterflies. Served him right.'

'And there's a snow dog,' added Audmund. Vargon

glared at him again, but the augurer pretended not to notice. 'It was thought to be a myth, but now that Timber is in Grindlewood, rumours are rife once again about the Guardian Dog, the prophecy, all of it.'

Zora narrowed her eyes. 'Timber, so that's what he's called. Perhaps we should test this Timber and see what he's made of.'

'That's what I always said, my Queen,' said Bodric, but there was no sign of his confident swagger any more. She had not been as delighted to see her old buzzard pet as he had hoped. Zora merely sneered and kicked Bodric out of her way as she walked up and down the room. Then she turned with a swirl and stopped.

'I am going to terrify them, terrify them all!'

Ripley was eavesdropping behind the sofa. His spying hadn't yielded anything of interest lately, so he had to be careful or he could be considered worthless too. On top of that, Vargon had already threatened to turn him into a fur collar for his cape, simply for being in the manor at all. The squirrel's tummy was doing cartwheels at the thought of what might happen to him. He didn't dare speak or move. He hardly dared to breathe.

Audmund was glad to finally reach the quiet of his study after another of Zora's rants. He took four pages out of a drawer. 'These are all I need,' he thought. 'It won't be long now.' He frowned and muttered as he studied them, looking up various books to check details and meanings. After a couple of hours of work, his eyes were sore and his head was spinning. He was about to put the pages back in the drawer, when he stopped. 'Vargon might search my room with his undetectable Searching spell.' He gazed around the study with his bulbous eyes, raised his wand towards his chest and mumbled a few words. 'That will do nicely,' he thought, then he tucked the pages into his cloak, safe inside a new secret pocket.

Vargon went to bed as soon as Zora had returned to her room. He was worn out. The task of bringing Zora back had taken two decades of hard work, and hiding out in such a fragile dimension had drained him even more. He often relied on strange mixtures of poison and other horrid potions just to keep going and appear stronger than he felt.

He lay down on his bed, tired and frustrated. After

spending all his life trying to discover all the Wandeleis' secrets, he hadn't really come up with much. His devotion to Zora had interrupted that work too. He had expected her to be a little different after all those years locked away, but she was proving to be difficult and reckless. He shuddered to think what she would be like when fully restored. And after all he'd done for her, she hadn't even thanked him. He let out a long disappointed sigh.

Back in Grindlewood garden, Luke and Jamie were in the fairy house doing puzzles. Abigail was in the house with Jemima when the butterflies arrived with another message.

> *The danger is growing, the evil is coming,*
> *You must prepare for the worst!*
> *You have to stop this sorceress,*
> *Or all in her path will be cursed!*

'What?' cried Jamie. 'I thought we just had to get the key.'

'Come on,' said Luke. 'We'd better tell the girls.'

Chapter Seven

THE QUEEN'S SECRETS

Queen Wanda woke suddenly, sensing trouble. She sent her fairies to raise the alarm and quickly dressed. Hurrying down the tunnel towards the vault, she met Pendrick along the way. They exchanged worried looks and ran on together.

When they reached the vault, they found Phineas in a heap by the open door. He had been so overcome by the Obedience spell that Audmund decided to leave him behind in case he hindered their escape. Wanda rushed inside and saw what she feared: the silver key was gone, and the WABOM had been moved. Pendrick examined the WABOM. He frowned. Two more pages had been torn out of *The Book of Darkness*.

The fairies arrived and attended to the spellbound

augurer. Wanda hurried back to her chamber, where Flint and Sparks joined her.

'Professor Allnutt is on his way,' said Sparks.

'How could anyone break into the vault?' asked Flint. 'We had such an elaborate set of charms around it.'

'And we changed them often,' said Sparks.

'This is the work of another traitor,' said Wanda. 'Someone who knew how to get around the sequence of charms because he knew what they were.'

'I hope that'll narrow down the list of suspects,' said Pendrick, entering the chamber.

Wanda sat down at her desk, tapping her fingers, thinking. 'Audmund is behind this,' she said after a moment. 'He must be. The third traitor let him in, and –'

Thaddeus Allnutt burst into the chamber, having come straight from the scene of the crime. 'Your Majesty, gentlemen,' he said. 'The fairies confirmed that Phineas is under the influence of an Obedience spell *and* a Block-out spell. He must have assisted the thief without knowing what he was doing.'

'Just as I thought,' said Wanda.

'How awful,' said Sparks. 'Phineas will be so upset.'

'More pages are missing from *The Book of Darkness*,' said Pendrick, 'two more pages from the Verses of Doom in the Chapter of the Dead.'

'Oh, no!' cried Flint, turning pale. 'That frightful spell uses so much dark magic.'

'It will take a terrible toll on whoever performs it,' said Sparks.

'But more importantly, who is being brought back from the dead?' asked Thaddeus. 'It's not the same as using *The Book of Light*, when one life is exchanged for another.'

'No,' said Wanda. 'The Verses of Doom only bring back the most dreaded evil.'

The professors waited patiently for instructions.

'We shall meet back here in one hour,' said Wanda after a pause. 'I want you to keep an eye on Phineas, Professor Flint. Try to undo any remnants of those charms and see if he can tell us anything useful.' Flint bowed and left. 'Professor Sparks, go to the vault and bring me the two remaining keys: the crystal key and the iron key, and the WABOM. Change the Locking charms – and make them stronger.' Sparks also bowed and hurried off. 'Pendrick, I want the security throughout Hollow Hill doubled. Organise the high-ranking wizards and witches and see to it immediately. I have already asked Lotus to send more butterflies to Grindlewood garden.'

Thaddeus looked at her, alarm spreading across his face.

Wanda motioned to him to sit down as Pendrick headed out. 'Have you any news for me, Thaddeus?'

'A little, Your Majesty,' he replied. 'As you requested, I looked into Zora's old tutor, Lord Vargon. His background is rather worrying.'

'Tell me everything.'

'He was a cunning warlock, very skilled. He befriended Worfeus and Zora's father, King Worfagus II, who trusted Vargon to educate both his children equally, but Vargon favoured Zora. He spotted her talent for the dark arts and encouraged her from an early age.'

'Do you think Vargon is behind Zora's return?' asked Wanda.

'I have no doubt,' said Thaddeus. 'Vargon went into hiding soon after Zora vanished. He could have been planning it for a long time.'

'Why is Audmund involved?'

'Audmund's great-grandmother was a Worfagon

witch,' said Thaddeus. 'That makes him just about acceptable to Vargon. He is also cunning, devious, and an expert in potion making and other strange concoctions, including poisons. Some of his skills will be needed to bring Zora back to full strength. In any case, his loyalty was always questionable. It must have been easy for him to switch sides.'

'But what would Audmund want in exchange?' asked the queen.

'Power, perhaps?'

Wanda looked into the distance, taking in all the information. 'They must not get the four keys – the gold, the crystal, the silver and the iron – whatever they are planning.'

Thaddeus looked troubled, but the queen understood his concern. 'You know the children and Timber must be involved. They are part of the prophecy.'

'Yes,' said Thaddeus. 'But my granddaughter …'

'I know,' said Wanda gently. 'But they are the *worthy*, chosen to come to our aid when our magical world comes to the brink of destruction.'

'Is it really that bad?' Have you had another vision?'

'Only blurred, foggy images,' said Wanda. 'But

Queen Lyra warned me that a terrible storm was coming. She felt it in her roots.'

'Extraordinary,' said Thaddeus.

They sat thoughtfully for a few minutes.

'We will prepare the children as best we can, but only as much as we are allowed,' said Wanda.

'Of course,' said Thaddeus.

'What about Mr and Mrs Grindle?' asked Wanda.

'As it happens, Greg and Gloria have gone to visit our friend the Wizard Peabody. I haven't managed to contact him myself yet. He is dreadful about answering his telephone, and mobile phones don't work near magic or magical people, so I don't know what this business is about. Something to do with Greg's great-uncle George, but I expect Peabody will keep them busy for a few weeks rather than days. He always goes into enormous detail and mounds of paperwork for even the smallest matter.'

'Good,' said Wanda. 'It's best if the children's parents aren't around for the quest. We don't want to have to use too much memory mist on them.'

'I'll let you know if Peabody turns up anything interesting,' said Thaddeus. 'Esther and I will be staying at the house, Abigail too, and Luke. His parents have gone to a family gathering, but Luke managed to avoid it, without my intervening. I also paid a visit to their school. I fixed it so that everyone will think the four children are there as normal, for a while at least.'

'That must have been tricky,' said Wanda.

'It was,' said Thaddeus, peering over his spectacles. 'Please don't ask.'

'Come over here,' said Wanda. 'I want to show you something.' They went over to her desk. 'I've been working on a complex puzzle. Queen Lyra started it and I promised her I would finish it.'

'Intriguing,' said Thaddeus, as he looked at the piles of parchment spread out on her desk.

'It's a giant encrypted puzzle, within which lies a map – a map with directions to Othelia's Orb.'

'Oh, my,' whispered Thaddeus. 'So it could be found again, after all this time.'

'Only if we can solve it.'

The children were walking slowly out to the garden, making sure that Jemima didn't fall. She was walking very gingerly on her crutches, but her ankle was already improving. It was the first dry day in weeks and the only one during their mid-term break so far.

'Whoa!' cried Luke. 'That's more butterflies than we've ever seen!'

Dozens of rainbow butterflies were flying around the garden, over the hedges and trees and even the house. Two of them landed on Timber's head, the third on Abigail. 'We have to go to Hollow Hill,' she said.

Timber bounded down the garden to tell the others. The children were wondering what to do about Jemima. They didn't like leaving her behind.

'My ankle is a bit better,' she said, seeing the looks on their faces. 'But I can't walk that far, not on crutches. Go and come back quickly. I'm dying to know what's going on.'

'Are you sure you don't mind?' asked Abigail.

'I'll be fine,' said Jemima.

Timber kept barking.

'He's really keen to get going,' said Jamie. 'We'd better hurry.'

Jemima walked slowly back inside, feeling just a little bit sorry for herself. Teddy followed her to keep her company. In the garden, some of the animals went to their lookout posts, while others went about their business. All of them were eager to hear the news from Hollow Hill.

❧

The three children and Timber hurried along the tunnels. Professor Pendrick met them at the reception chamber.

'Hello, everyone,' he said. 'I take it Jemima is resting. Come along, the queen and Professor Allnutt are waiting.'

The queen explained about the second theft. 'Your quest to find one key is now a quest to find two keys and the missing pages.'

Before anyone could ask any more about it, Jamie blurted out his thoughts. 'We had two more messages from the butterflies,' he said. 'One said *we* had to stop Zora, and the other said something about a *special dog*. What's this really about?'

Thaddeus turned slowly and looked at the queen over his spectacles, which were perched on the end of his nose. He wasn't sure how much the queen wanted them to know just yet.

'I will deal with Zora,' said the queen. 'Timber is a very special dog, a malamute and a snow dog. Snow dogs have often played a special role in our past.'

'Oh?' said Jamie.

Wanda gestured to everyone to sit down as Lotus brought in trays of Calming lemonade. Then she explained.

'Long ago, the Ancients were the only people to possess magic. When the time came for them to move on to another world, they passed that gift to us, their chosen people. They laid down rules about how their magic should be used and how we should make amends if those rules were broken – or face dire consequences.'

'What if something wasn't your fault?' asked Luke. 'Accidents can happen.'

'In our world, all wrongs must be put right,' said Wanda. 'The universe decides when.'

Luke frowned as he tried to make sense of it. Abigail was listening intently but Jamie still looked frustrated.

'You have heard of Tyrus. He was once Grindlewood's protector,' said Wanda. 'There were others too, all wolves. Now Timber is here. He is the first malamute to protect Grindlewood. I have explained it to him.'

'But how could he protect the whole place?' said Jamie. 'That's impossible.'

'He is a promise from the Ancients to help us put right all the wrongs of the past. He is a guardian, a protector and a symbol for good,' said Wanda.

'I still don't get it,' said Jamie crossly.

'He will have a special role to play in saving our future,' said Wanda. 'But we do not know how events will unfold.'

Jamie stroked his dog, who looked at him lovingly. He seemed calmer now, glad that he wasn't keeping any secrets from Jamie.

The meeting was cut short by Sparks. 'Apologies, Your Majesty, Professor, everyone. We are ready for the first demonstration.'

The queen nodded to Sparks and stood up. 'I must check on the new compass brooch,' she said. 'The quest will begin once the brooch has been successfully tested, so please be ready to return here quickly when we send word. Professor Allnutt has arranged for you to be absent from school without any questions being asked.'

Normally, holidays from school would have been exciting, but the children felt this quest was starting off rather strangely. They hoped they would know a lot more before they set off with the new compass brooch.

❧

Queen Wanda and Thaddeus worked late into the night.

'What is it, Thaddeus?' said the queen. She could tell something was niggling at him.

'Your Majesty, Tyrus lost his life protecting Queen Lyra and many others died by his side.'

'I cannot change what is meant to be,' said Wanda. 'Our murky past has caught up with us and I have the responsibility to ensure that we make amends. The children and Timber are here to help us save ourselves and Grindlewood.'

Thaddeus looked troubled. 'But Your Majesty, our magic isn't back to normal yet and it will be some time before we can do the Renewal charm properly. We can try on midsummer's night, although Halloween is always best, but it's only March now. Then there's Zora, Vargon, Audmund and goodness knows who else is involved. It's a lot to expect of them, worthy or not.'

'The children will not do this alone,' said Wanda firmly. 'I will do everything in my power to keep them safe but we must put everything right, Thaddeus. It is our sworn promise.'

Thaddeus knew Wanda spoke the truth, but if Timber truly was the Guardian of Grindlewood, their enemies would come to know that too.

Chapter Eight

KIDNAPPED

The next day, Jemima managed to walk slowly all the way down the garden to the fairy house, on her own and without much discomfort. She was excited to check out a box of oddments her father had found in the cellar.

Abigail popped up through the trap door after her spell classes in Hollow Hill. Timber and Teddy came in to say hello after their patrol. Teddy hopped onto Jemima's lap and Timber sat on the floor. The boys would join them after their fencing practice in the barn. The sky was very dark and peels of thunder rumbled overhead.

'This is the stuff my dad found,' said Jemima, rummaging in a large cardboard box on the table. She pulled out two scarves, one woolly hat, a mouldy leather glove, a couple of old photoframes, a tatty notebook, a bent quill, bottles of ink, a brass clock and a very old stamp collection in several albums.

'The stamps look interesting,' said Abigail. 'They're very unusual.'

'What about this!' cried Jemima, pulling something out from the very bottom of the box.

'A wand!' whispered Abigail.

'Do you think it's real?' asked Jemima.

'It looks real,' said Abigail.

'I wonder who it belonged to,' said Jemima. 'Did Great-Great-Uncle George own it, use it, or did he just hide it? Or maybe he was a wand maker. What do you think, Abi?'

'He could have found it somewhere,' said Abigail, taking it in her hand. 'You have to be careful with wands. The wand chooses the owner, not the other way around. You should never steal one.' She gave it back to her friend.

Jemima waved it and flicked it like a real witch would. 'I'd really like to know how it ended up here.'

'Granddad might be able to find out,' said Abigail. 'We should tell him about it anyway.'

'Speaking of wands,' said Jemima, 'show me what you learned today.'

Abigail liked to practise new spells with Jemima. She knew her friend would be excited, even if Abigail didn't get the spell absolutely right. The latest lesson was how to move small objects around, tie a scarf or shoelaces, and heat up liquids that had gone cold. She tested her new skills on the hot chocolate her mum had left in the fairy house for them.

Jemima tasted it. 'Yum! Perfect!'

'There's one more,' said Abigail. 'Granddad taught me this one at home. It's called the Reversing spell.'

Jemima watched as Abigail flicked the wand and undid the laces she had just tied.

'That's clever,' said Jemima.

'It only reverses spells that have just been cast,' said Abigail. 'It'll be a while before I learn the more powerful spells.'

Jemima picked up the wand and waved it around again, trying to imagine what it would be like to cast spells. Suddenly, there was a very bright flash followed by several loud bangs of thunder. The rain pelted down and the wind slammed against the windows.

'Ooops! I hope I didn't do that!' said Jemima. They

both giggled and looked towards the crooked side window. The weather was turning very wild. Both Timber and Teddy jumped to attention. Something wasn't right.

There were more claps of thunder, louder this time, and right overhead. Suddenly, the door and windows burst open and a rush of wind entered the fairy house. Timber barked and stomped around the table. Teddy's fur stood on end as Jemima held him tightly, thinking he might be frightened.

Books, comics, hats and scarves and all the contents of the cardboard box blew around in the mini storm that enveloped them. Even the heavy old books fell off their shelves as the bookcase rocked against the wall. The whirlwind strengthened till it shook the whole fairy house, then whipped into a tight vortex in one corner of the room. Spikes of lightning shot like arrows through the whirlwind, then curved and spun red, and redder still, and then ...

... Zora stood there, a gloating smile stretched across her thin, bony face. In that split second of surprise, she reached out and pulled Jemima and Teddy straight into the vortex. Timber lunged forward to stop them being sucked away, but he too was caught in the whirling mass, and in another bright flash, all three were taken.

The wind and rain stopped and it was very still and quiet. Abigail struggled to catch her breath, then she let out a piercing scream that even the boys heard over in the barn. They hurried over, their rapiers still in their hands. The fairy house door had fallen off and the whole room was in a terrible mess.

'What happened?' cried Jamie, looking around. 'Where's Jemima, and Timber, and Teddy?'

Esther burst out of the kitchen and ran down the garden.

'They're gone!' screamed Abigail. 'She took them!'

Esther looked at the shower of red dust on the floor as she held her daughter close to her. She uttered only one word: 'Zora.'

When Jemima, Timber and Teddy arrived in Mord Manor, the whirlwind dropped them in a heap in the corridor of the dungeon, then vanished. Zora stood nearby, fixing them with an ice-cold stare.

Teddy and Timber were quickly whooshed into a cell by four burly warlocks. Jemima was still struggling

to get to her feet when she was hoisted off the floor by two guards who then flung her into the same cell. They slammed the door behind her, securing it with a spell. Determined to keep back any tears or feelings of squeamishness, Jemima checked the animals were OK. Then she checked her tender ankle. As she stood up to test it, she realised that she still had the wand in her hand. She was holding it along the shaft of one of the crutches and no one had noticed it. 'Lucky!' she thought. Timber licked her hand and then nosed the wand – they mustn't let the Worfagons see it.

Zora marched off to find Vargon, delighted with herself for making such a bold move so soon after her return. 'I not only captured the girl, but the big dog as well, and a horrid little cat,' she announced to her shocked tutor.

'You should have spoken to me first, Zora,' said Vargon.

'Address me as "Your Redness".'

'That is not important,' said Vargon. 'What is it about you and your brother that you always have to show off?'

'I am not like my brother!'

'We have a plan, Zora,' said Vargon, ignoring her

outrage. 'But Audmund decides to snatch two keys, and then you go and grab that girl and her pets. Really, I cannot have you both messing up my plan!'

'*Improving* your plan!' roared Zora. 'You said the children and the dog are important to the Forest Queen.'

'I don't like having *that dog* here,' said Vargon.

'What do you mean?' asked Zora.

'He's not like other dogs. He's different, powerful. He's ... he's like the snow dogs mentioned in the prophecy.'

'If he's important, he's useful,' cried Zora. 'As for the prophecy, isn't it all mumbo jumbo?'

'If any bit of the prophecy is true, he could be a danger to us,' said Vargon.

'Danger?' said Zora, sneering. 'Nothing will stop me once I am restored. I will perform and withstand powerful magic. I will crush any resistance. I will rule as the Red Queen and no prophecy, or dog, will stop me!'

Vargon banged his stick on the ground. 'You have the same arrogance as your brother had, and that was his downfall. As for your prisoners, they will only be a nuisance. Now go and lie down – you look dreadful.

You used too much magic shunting to Grindlewood without a portal. It was foolish, rash and disobedient.'

Zora stood there fuming, her face twisted and bitter. 'I am not the little girl you used to teach, tutor,' she said through her teeth. 'It is *you* who must obey *me* now.'

Vargon did not want to continue arguing. He wasn't feeling too well himself. 'There are only two things we *must* do,' he said, slowly and carefully. 'First, we must restore you to full power, then we must find the orb. If the Wandeleis find it first, they may decide to unleash its power and destroy us.'

'I thought you said they were too peace-loving to fight,' said Zora. 'Anyway, they will be no match for me, especially if I get it first.'

'Nothing is certain yet,' said Vargon. 'And I'm sure they will defend themselves if we start any trouble.'

'Everything all right?' asked Audmund, popping his head around the doorway.

'Just another interruption to my carefully orchestrated plan,' said Vargon. 'Come along, Audmund, you might as well meet our new guests.'

The three of them headed down to the dungeon.

Jemima looked around the cell. It was very bare,

with only a stool in one corner and a raggy mat in another – nowhere to hide the wand. She tried stuffing it down one leg of her trousers but it didn't stay in place when she moved even the slightest bit. She heard footsteps, voices. People were coming. Leaning on her crutch, she felt a little panicked. She couldn't let anyone take the wand. Timber grabbed one of the crutches in his teeth. Jemima suddenly knew what he meant.

'Yes! Clever dog!' She held the crutch steady and pushed the wand into a cavity just below the handle. 'Let's hope they don't think of looking in there.' She eased herself down onto the floor again, and pulled Teddy onto her lap. Timber stood beside her, growling, ready for whatever or whoever was coming.

Esther sent Nura Nightingale to Hollow Hill to let the queen know what had happened and then to spread the word around the village. There was shock in the garden as everyone wondered what to do.

'Kidnapped?' said Dougal.

'I'm afraid so,' said Oberon.

'What? Who? And how?' asked Eldric.

'Only a Worfagon could have shunted in like that and left so quickly,' said Gildevard.

'Um, what does that mean?' asked Dougal.

'Shunting is when magical people move from one dimension to another,' said Oberon.

'It's complicated magic,' said Gildevard. 'Wandeleis avoid it because it is very dark, but that never bothered the Worfagons.'

'It's the reason they look so wretched,' said Oberon. 'Dark magic comes at a price.'

'Why didn't they take Abigail?' asked Ramona.

'She was lucky,' said the eagle.

'Timber and Teddy must have tried to save Jemima,' said Dougal.

No one said anything for a moment. They suddenly felt lost without Timber.

'How do we find them and get them back?' asked Cindy.

'Esther sent word to Hollow Hill,' said Oberon. 'The queen will think of something.'

'I can hear them talking about red dust on the floor,' said the eagle. 'Abigail has described a frightful woman in red. Strange that Zora came herself.'

The others looked horrified.

'Thank you, Gildevard. There's no need to worry everyone even more,' said Oberon. 'We must carry out Timber's last instructions.'

'Guard the garden and stay alert,' said the Brigadier.

'That's right,' said the owl.

'I'm going to take a look,' said Gildevard, and he flew off. The owl followed him to the windowsill of the fairy house. Dougal and Trigger trotted inside and sniffed around. The foxes and Ramona waited outside on the porch.

'This is abominable!' cried Pendrick. Three professors had just arrived through the trap door. Pendrick waved his wand to try to detect as much information as possible, but it just fizzed and blew a puff of smoke.

'Everything is so unstable,' muttered Flint.

'We should have been more careful,' said Thaddeus. 'More guards, more Protection charms, something.'

'I'm not sure they would have stopped this,' said Pendrick, stepping over some debris.

'Abigail was in the room when it happened,' said Esther.

'Oh, my dear, are you all right?' asked Thaddeus.

'What'll happen to Jemima, Teddy and Timber?' asked Abigail.

'Is this about Timber again?' asked Jamie. 'Is that why they were kidnapped?'

'We can't be sure of anything, Jamie,' said Esther. 'We don't even know where they are, do we, Thaddeus?'

Abigail's granddad shook his head.

'What about the red dust?' said Luke. 'That's got to be Zora. We've seen red streaks in the sky since we first heard her name, and in the last few days, even the puddles looked red.'

'Jemima's already injured,' said Jamie, fighting back tears of worry, anger and frustration.

'Timber won't let anything happen to her,' said Thaddeus.

'And what about Timber and Teddy?' asked Jamie.

'Jemima's crutches are missing,' said Luke, interrupting. He looked under the overturned table and chairs, and checked behind the bookcase. 'They're definitely not here.'

'Jemima had a wand in her hand when Zora grabbed her,' said Abigail.

'What wand?' asked Esther.

'It was in a box of old things that her dad found in the cellar,' said Abigail.

'The cellar,' repeated Thaddeus quietly. Pendrick gave him a funny look.

'What about the compass brooch?' asked Esther. 'Could it find them?'

'It's worth a try,' said Thaddeus. 'Sparks is doing some final adjustments, although, maybe, hmm, it might work.' He scribbled down a few symbols and other illegible scrawls on a loose sheet of paper that had blown around in the whirlwind. 'Pendrick, I need to talk to Sparks right away. Meet me in the Deliberation Room when you and Esther are finished here.'

Thaddeus hugged his granddaughter then he and Flint left for Hollow Hill. Pendrick and Esther continued inspecting the fairy house, then used whatever magic they could muster to repair the damage.

❧

Timber and Teddy heard them first. Then Jemima heard the tap-tapping of Zora's boots until the sound stopped right outside her cell door. Zora peered in the barred window. Something in particular caught her eye. She cocked her head to one side and stared at Jemima, who was terrified that somehow the sorceress had figured out what she was hiding.

Zora unlocked the door and marched inside. Audmund and Vargon followed. Timber growled but stayed close to Jemima. Teddy hissed and wriggled about as Jemima held him firmly.

'I'm surprised,' said Zora, after a long stare. 'He's quite a handsome dog.'

Timber responded with a louder growl, as Zora circled her prisoners.

'All dogs are trouble,' said Audmund. Timber's growls turned to barks as he remembered Audmund from the battle in Bodric's Gorge.

'Never forget history, Audmund,' said Vargon, stomping into the cell, his stick pounding extra loudly on the stone floor, his cloak twirling behind him.

'I'm more interested in the future, My Lord,' said Audmund. 'I agree with Her Redness that the dog may be of value, but that cat certainly isn't.' Teddy hissed at him and Timber bared his teeth again.

'Quiet!' roared Vargon. He looked directly at Jemima. 'Your name?'

'Jemima.'

'Tell us what the Forest Queen is up to, pretty little girl.'

'Um, what?' said Jemima.

'What has she told you about the orb?' said Vargon.

Jemima just stared at him.

'What has the Forest Queen been saying? We know you visit her, you and those other do-gooder children and your furry pets. What do you talk about? Answer me!'

'Is she pretty, Vargon?' asked Zora. 'Is that what people call pretty, nowadays?' She grabbed some of Jemima's hair and considered the shiny blonde curls. Vargon huffed and puffed, frustrated by the interruption. Audmund rolled his eyes and moved slowly towards the door. He had a feeling this interview was going to be mostly about Zora. He was right.

'Why do you think she's pretty, Vargon? She has blonde, curly hair and bright blue eyes. When was that ever pretty?' Zora let go of Jemima's hair after giving it a sharp tug and circled her again. She looked her up and down, making odd faces as she considered her prettiness. 'I suppose she could be called pretty, in a different sort of way. I was always called pretty when I was a girl. Perhaps I need more potion, something to restore my youth and loveliness. See to it, Audmund.'

'Right away,' said Audmund and he left immediately.

'It really doesn't matter if she's pretty or not,' said Vargon. 'You should ...'

'And she has a bandage on her leg,' said Zora, ignoring him. 'Tut tut!'

'Bah!' cried Vargon. 'This is hopeless.' He turned towards the door. 'Guards! Separate these prisoners. I don't want them getting up to any devilment. Move the dog to the big cell and the cat to the small one. Leave the girl here.'

'Yes, My Lord,' they replied together, and they entered the cell.

'Remember, Timber and cat,' said Vargon from the doorway. 'If you misbehave, your pretty little mistress will pay the price.' Then he turned to Zora. 'Go to your room and drink some more potion, before you undo any more of your recovery.' He turned and stomped off down the corridor.

Zora didn't argue this time as she was feeling rather woozy. All she could muster was a red-eyed glare. She gave Jemima's curls one last tug before she left the cell, while the guards struggled with Timber. The dog wasn't happy about leaving Jemima alone, but he didn't have much choice. He knew Vargon would carry out his threat if either he or Teddy caused trouble. The guards dragged him into another cell and slammed the door shut. There was a mournful meow as Teddy was snatched by the scruff of the neck and flung into the smaller cell.

'Are you all right, Teddy?' barked Timber.

'I'm fine,' he meowed back. 'I'm so cross. How are we going to get out of here?'

'We'll think of something.'

The guards slammed Jemima's door shut, and locked it with a spell. She sat there alone, wondering what to do. She checked the wand – it was still in place. She tested her ankle again – it didn't feel too bad, considering all the shoving and pushing. She looked around; she was stuck in a cell, somewhere probably not on any ordinary map, with no way to get home, and Timber and Teddy had been taken away from her. Did anyone know where they were? A couple of tears fell down her cheeks. Then she got cross with herself. 'They'll come for us, I know they will. Jamie, Luke,

Abigail and the professors, they'll find us, somehow.'
For a while, Timber's howling was comforting, but
even that had to stop when the guards warned him
to be quiet. Then it was really quiet — quiet, lonely
and scary.

⁖

The butterflies flew into the garden with another
message, but strangely, it was the same one as before:

> *The danger is growing, the evil is coming,*
> *You must prepare for the worst!*
> *You have to stop this sorceress,*
> *Or all in her path will be cursed!*

'Maybe they thought we weren't listening the
first time,' said Luke.

'As if we needed to hear that twice,' said Jamie. 'I
mean, why can't they tell us something useful?'

Oberon flew over and landed on Jamie's
shoulder. The owl rubbed his beak on the
back of his neck, hoping to soothe him.
Dougal and Trigger trotted over to give
what comfort they could, licking and

~ 97 ~

nuzzling his hands, just like Timber used to.

'Luke,' said Jamie. 'What am I going to tell Mum and Dad?'

Chapter Nine

THE DIMLOCK

Bodric fluttered outside Timber's cell window. 'Well, well, look who's got a new kennel, I mean prison cell!'

'YOU!' barked Timber.

'Do you know where you are, big doggy?' The buzzard didn't wait for a reply. 'Mord Manor – my new home. This grand mansion belongs to Lord Vargon, Zora's powerful tutor, guardian, and now her saviour too.'

'You wouldn't be so brave if this door wasn't here,' said Timber.

Bodric shuddered at the thought. He flew off, chortling to himself, delighted to see Timber and Teddy locked up and out of reach. Timber stomped around his cell for hours, longing to howl. Eventually, he sat down opposite the door, staring at it as if willing it to open.

He didn't have a plan and neither did Teddy. Waiting around for something to happen was so frustrating. There was nothing to be seen and nothing to be heard, not until the following night.

It was late. After another row with Vargon, Zora was too fidgety to sleep. She decided to visit the dungeon and take another look at the so-called pretty prisoner. Timber heard her coming down the stairs, along one corridor, then the next. Zora's newest boots were even louder than the last pair. Timber sat to attention, hoping to hear something useful. He was in luck.

'Vargon treats me like a child!' she proclaimed to no one at all. 'But I will storm the Wandeleis' stronghold and destroy that Forest Queen, and when I have the orb, I will absorb its power, so no one else can have it. My revenge will be complete when I am the undisputed ruler of Worfagonia. It will be sweet. It will be magnificent. *I* will be magnificent!'

She turned the corner and walked straight into Vargon. He had been standing there so quietly even Timber and Teddy hadn't heard him.

'Zora, my dear,' he said. 'Of course you will have your sweet revenge, but if the Forest Queen has the orb and you destroy her hideout, it will be lost to us forever.'

'She couldn't be that foolish, and stop telling me what to do, Vargon! I'm a grown woman now and –'

'And when have I ever misguided you?'

'When you didn't stop my brother from banishing me!'

'No one expected that, not even your father.'

'How dare you speak of him!'

Zora's eyes were blazing red but Vargon was determined to keep cool. 'I will find this orb and it shall be my gift to you,' he said, trying to tempt her. 'After that, you can destroy whatever and whomever you wish. Remember, the sooner you are restored, the sooner your fun begins.'

Once again, Zora's rage used up most of her energy. She glowered at Jemima through the barred window, but didn't enter. Vargon escorted her back down the corridor and she went to her room. He returned to his study and his research on the orb. A long time ago, he had heard mention of a map and four keys from a wandering seer, but he wasn't sure if what he had been told was true. Seers often told lies for a reward in gold.

Timber curled up in a corner of his cell, wondering how he could warn the queen about what he had just heard. Later in the night, he was just about to finally fall asleep when he heard a scurrying noise. It stopped outside his cell. He listened and waited. There was another little scurry, then it stopped again. Only one animal moved like that without any scent – Ripley.

'Is that you, squirrel?' Timber growled under the door. 'Are you scheming with Bodric?'

There was no reply. Ripley couldn't decide if he wanted to talk to Timber or not. He didn't like Mord Manor much, but he hadn't enjoyed life in Hollow Hill either. He had expected to find greater excitement and opportunity with the Worfagons, but it hadn't really turned out that way. He spent most of his time hiding or worrying, whenever he wasn't spying for them, and now that Zora was back, everything felt so downright scary.

Suddenly it occurred to Timber that perhaps Ripley wanted to talk to him but was afraid of being overheard. He was also afraid of Timber.

'Ripley, is that you? Answer me now or go away!'

'Yes, yes, it's me, but be quiet,' said the squirrel. 'I don't want to get caught down here.'

The children weren't very hungry. As they pushed and poked at their supper, the phone rang in the hall.

'Let me talk to your parents first,' said Thaddeus. 'I know a Voice charm that will make them believe they have spoken to Jemima.'

When Thaddeus eventually called him to the phone, Jamie quickly realised that his father didn't really hear a word he said. He looked a bit down when he returned to the kitchen.

'I'm sorry, Jamie, but we can't have your parents calling the police,' said Thaddeus. 'This is something the magical community has to fix.'

'Neither your parents nor the police can find Jemima, Timber and Teddy if magic has been used,' said Esther gently. 'It's better we do this our way.'

'Now, I must return to Hollow Hill,' said Thaddeus. 'Sparks is resetting the compass so it will lead us to the right place. We'll get them back. I promise.'

After the dreadful news about the kidnapping, everyone in Hollow Hill was busy with new orders and instructions. The queen wanted to see her professors again. Sparks was excused as he was finishing the compass.

'That was a daring move by Zora,' said Wanda. 'None of us expected anything quite like this.'

The others nodded and frowned; they should have expected it.

'A sample of the red dust showed traces of a powerful Restoration potion,' said Pendrick. 'Audmund's work. He was good at that sort of thing.'

'There's more bad news, Your Majesty,' said Thaddeus. 'Jemima had a wand in her hand when Zora whirled in and grabbed her. I'm sorry I didn't know about this wand earlier, or I would have made sure of its origins.'

'Any idea who it belonged to?' asked Flint.

'No,' said Thaddeus.

'Ahem, about Timber,' said Flint. 'Do the Worfagons believe the prophecy?'

'Few of them respect the Ancients and their prophecies the way we do,' said Wanda.

'Vargon might,' said Pendrick. 'He came from an old school of sorcery, full of traditional teachings, superstitions, and also prophecies. If he doesn't believe the prophecy about the dog, he'll be wary of it. He won't do anything rash.'

'But taking Jemima, Timber and Teddy was rash,' said Flint.

'Yes,' said Thaddeus. 'It doesn't quite add up. Perhaps Zora has other ideas.'

'And Audmund?' said Flint.

'He's a traitor, a spy, a potion maker and a thief,' said Pendrick crossly.

'Dear me,' sighed Thaddeus. 'Everything has become so complicated.'

Sparks burst in. 'It's ready!'

The children were called to Hollow Hill immediately. Esther came with them, Oberon, Dougal and Trigger too. They met the queen and the professors in the Deliberation Room.

'What is this place?' asked Jamie, gazing around.

'It's where we design, make and test magical inventions,' said Esther.

It was a rectangular room with heavy old tables, long wooden workbenches and a variety of strange machines. Steam and smoke billowed out of potion pots and tubes, and the shelves that stood along every wall were packed with weird objects and instruments.

'Using Professor Allnutt's idea,' said Sparks, 'I was able to modify the new compass brooch for our, eh, your new task. By the way, it isn't a brooch this time, it's a locket. Take a look.' He turned to the table beside him, which was covered in odd bits of metal, wire and glass, and he picked out a gold locket. It hung on a gold chain and was about the size of a flattened egg. Covered with tiny engravings and magical symbols, it looked antique and expensive. 'This is the Dimension Locket,' Sparks said, holding it up proudly. 'DimLock for short. It will take you through a portal to the location where Jemima, Timber and Teddy are being held.'

'What portal?' asked Jamie.

'The one in Grindlewood Forest,' said Thaddeus.

'There's a portal in our forest?' said Jamie.

'More than one,' said Thaddeus.

'Another secret,' whispered Luke.

'Why do we need a portal?' said Jamie. 'Zora just zoomed in and out.'

'Because it's a Worfagon dimension, and we haven't mastered the art of shunting the way the Worfagons have,' said Pendrick uncomfortably. 'And we don't really want to.'

'Shunting to Worfagon dimensions can be very dangerous,' said Flint, then immediately wished he hadn't said anything.

'Dangerous?' said Luke.

'He means it is a dangerous and unpredictable way for *magical* people to travel,' said Thaddeus.

'The way our magic is at the moment, we might even explode,' added Sparks.

'What about Abi?' cried Jamie. 'She's a Wandelei.'

'Abigail has not reached qualification level yet,' said Sparks, 'so she will not explode.'

'Thank you, Sparks,' said Pendrick, frowning.

Thaddeus sighed rather loudly.

'The augurers are in a trance at the moment, checking the location again,' said Wanda. 'Once they confirm it, we will enchant the DimLock and you will take it to the portal.'

'Like the Brooch of Balmedoch, it's easy to use,' said Sparks. 'When you are at the portal, you all hold hands – and hold the animals, of course – open the locket and whoosh, you are away! When you want to come back, you gather at the same portal you arrived at, close the locket and you will return to the portal in the forest.'

'There is one more important thing to remember,' said Pendrick. He turned to his colleague. 'Professor Sparks?'

The children looked from Pendrick to Sparks, back

and forth. They both seemed reluctant to say what this important thing was.

'I had to remodel the DimLock in a hurry,' said Sparks, apologetically. 'It will take you to your destination, but it will whisk you back after no more than five minutes. When you come back, I'll finish correcting that prob –'

Before the children could protest, Lotus hurried in with a message from the augurers.

'They're in Mord Manor, Your Majesty,' she said. 'Vargon's private dimension.'

'Oh, that'll be tricky,' said Sparks. 'I'm afraid you'll only have two or three minutes in that place.'

'Private dimension?' said Abigail.

'What?' cried Jamie. 'How do we rescue them in two or three minutes?'

'Is it two, or three?' asked Luke, looking at his watch.

'I know it's very little time,' said Sparks, 'but that dimension is dreadfully unstable. I would need a few weeks to adjust the DimLock so that –'

'Pendrick, take the locket to the augurers,' said Wanda. 'Oversee the enchantment and bring it back right away.'

Pendrick took the locket, and he and Lotus left the room.

'Abigail, you will wear the DimLock,' said Wanda. 'Good luck, children. Use your time wisely. Pendrick and Thaddeus will take you to the portal.'

Pendrick returned soon and they set off down the tunnels. Everyone looked nervous.

'We'll get them back,' said Jamie, trying to encourage himself and the others. 'We can do it. We just have to be quick, that's all.'

'Sure,' said Luke. 'We can get them out in, um, a couple of minutes, can't we?'

No one said anything else.

Chapter Ten

FIRST RESCUE

This time they took the tunnel to Grindlewood Forest. The children tried to prepare themselves for every possible outcome in the manor, but they really couldn't be sure what lay ahead. The professors listened anxiously to their chatter. They emerged a bit muddied as they squeezed out of the tunnel right in the centre of the forest, close to Worfeus' old lair.

'It's in the middle of those trees,' said Pendrick, pointing to a small circle of silver birch. They went over and looked around. It didn't look like much until Pendrick moved to the centre of the trees, bent down and rubbed away a layer of thick moss that was covering a smooth round stone. There were symbols engraved all over it.

'We never knew this was here,' said Jamie.

'Did Worfeus ever use it?' asked Luke.

'He could have,' said Thaddeus. 'But Worfeus wasn't known for his patience. He probably didn't try hard enough to find it.'

'Pay attention, everyone,' said Pendrick. He bent down and pressed three fingers into the markings on the stone, then stood up and began to chant. A wide ring of pale-blue light appeared and hovered over the stone, right in the midst of the trees. Thaddeus beckoned to the children and pets to come forward as Pendrick said the final words of the chant. He opened the locket hanging around Abigail's neck. They were just about to step onto the stone and into the blue light when Thaddeus pulled them back. Something was wrong. The light was wobbling and bubbling. It faded, then popped – gone.

'What happened?' cried Jamie.

'Something threw the portal off,' said Pendrick. The professors examined the circle. There were singe marks around the stone and some of the foliage nearby had turned black. The children stood by, watching anxiously. Trigger and Dougal were unusually quiet. Oberon was perched motionless on a branch nearby, intrigued by what was happening.

'I don't think it was the DimLock,' said Thaddeus.

'It's our magic, isn't it?' said Pendrick, looking at his friend.

Thaddeus nodded and closed the locket. 'Let's try again.'

Pendrick began the chant, louder this time, and Thaddeus joined in. It was an unusual harmony with an eerie ring to it, breaking through the silence of the forest. Oberon watched from a tree as the children stepped forward, the dogs beside them. The ring of blue light appeared, flickering, fading, flickering again. Then the light pulsed as Thaddeus and Pendrick switched to a different chant. They raised their wands and the light brightened – they were holding the portal open. Abigail opened the locket when her granddad gave her the slightest of nods, and the children and dogs stepped onto the stone and through the ring. The portal popped, and they vanished.

The DimLock was very accurate. They landed inside Timber's cell and he bounded over, smothering Jamie with licks and nuzzles. Trigger and Dougal were very excited though they had been warned not to bark. The blue ring of light was still there, but it pulsed unevenly.

'Quick, we don't have much time,' said Jamie.

Teddy meowed loudly in the next cell. Timber growled and began scratching at the door.

'It's OK, Timber, we can hear him too,' said Jamie.

The two boys stood either side of the barred window checking to see if anyone was coming from either direction, while Abigail tried a few different spells on the lock. It was a lot to hope for, but if they could open the locks quickly, they might just be able to get everyone out and be gone in a flash.

'One minute gone,' said Luke, checking his watch.

'Why won't one of these spells do something?' said Abigail.

The blue light was dimming.

'Two minutes,' said Luke.

All three dogs were getting very agitated and their growling was getting louder.

'We've got to go,' said Luke. 'If we don't, we'll be stuck here.'

'Come on, magic!' cried Jamie.

'I'm so sorry,' said Abigail.

'Hold the dogs, get ready to jump!' cried Luke. 'One! Two! Three, Jummmpppp!' Abigail shut the DimLock as they dived into the light.

'Jamie! I'm in here!' cried Jemima, from down the corridor.

'Jem-i-m-aaaaaaa!' cried Jamie, turning his head as he disappeared through the portal.

WHUMP!

They arrived on the forest floor. The dogs jumped up quickly and bounded around, barking with excitement. Thaddeus and Pendrick were thrown off their feet once the portal closed.

'Oh my! Hello, Timber,' said Thaddeus, as he received a generous lick. He picked himself off the ground and patted the dog. 'Well done, children, well done. Did you see Jemima and Teddy?'

'No, but we heard them,' said Jamie. 'We arrived in Timber's cell. Teddy seemed to be in the cell beside him, and we heard Jemima just as we were sucked back.'

'My spells were useless, Granddad,' said Abigail.

'I never expected you to undo a Worfagon spell in two minutes,' said Thaddeus. 'But it was worth a try. We'll practise again tonight.'

'Thank goodness you got Timber back,' said Pendrick. 'And the DimLock works. We can reset it and you can try again.'

There was a loud, creeping CRAAAAACK!

'What?'

'Oh, no!'

'NO!'

The portal stone cracked in half then broke into several pieces. The circle of trees looked like they had been hit by lightning.

'The dark magic of Vargon's dimension just killed the portal,' said Pendrick.

'As did our sick magic,' said Thaddeus. He scowled.

'Is there another one?' asked Luke.

Pendrick made a strange face.

'There are several portals,' said Thaddeus. 'But the queen must give permission to use them.'

'Where's the nearest one?' asked Jamie.

'I don't think we'll be using the nearest one,' said Thaddeus.

'Where is it?'

'In the garden.'

❦

Bodric and Ripley had shunt stones tied around their necks to allow them to hop dimensions whenever they were spying. Gildevard had spotted the stone around Bodric's neck when he found the buzzard snooping around Grindlewood Forest one day. It gave him an idea. He hid near the portal and waited patiently. When he saw Ripley approach it, he flew like a rocket, clamped on to the squirrel's back, and made it through the portal, much to Ripley's dismay.

'You'll get me into trouble,' cried Ripley, shaking the eagle off.

'Nonsense,' said Gildevard. 'I won't tell if you don't.'

'They'll know. Drat! Damn it!'

The eagle flew away leaving the squirrel to figure out what excuse he would give for letting someone hitch a ride to Vargon's private dimension.

It was risky for the eagle, but he was a very confident bird, confident enough to go uninvited to Mord Manor; confident enough to try to be Zora's new friend. He flew around the manor a couple of times, looking in the windows from a distance to get a sense of the place. When he found Zora's room, he landed on the sill. There was no mistaking it. The walls, the furnishings, her clothes, and most of her frizzy hair were all blood red.

He tapped lightly on the window with his beak, then flew back a little and performed an impressive flying display right outside her window. It had the desired effect. Zora moved closer to the window to watch. Twirling around, she left her room and marched downstairs to the parlour to make her next demand.

'I have decided that as queen I need a pet, one that befits my position.'

Vargon looked up slowly from his *Poisons Almanac*. Bodric was already fawning at her feet, hoping she was referring to him. But she ignored him.

'I want a golden eagle,' she said. 'A good choice for royalty, don't you think?'

'What nonsense is this?' roared Vargon. 'We had intruders in the manor and all you are concerned with is a royal pet!' His face was purple with rage.

'Did they take anything?' she asked.

'I'm waiting to hear from the dungeon commander.'

Then Audmund entered the room.

'My Lord, the commander had nothing further to add to his earlier report. Some children and two dogs shunted in, grabbed Timber and left,' he said. 'But we have another unexpected guest.'

'WHAT? Who?'

'A golden eagle,' said Audmund. 'I think I recognise him.'

'He must be the one I saw outside,' said Zora. 'I want that eagle, Audmund. Get him for me.' She swept out of the room, almost stepping on Bodric as she passed.

'Take heed, buzzard,' said Audmund, looking down at him. 'You might find you've been replaced if you're not careful.'

Bodric knew Audmund was right, and he was worried. He cowered behind an armchair as Vargon shuffled up and down the room, stomping his stick in irritation.

'The eagle might be useful,' said Audmund. 'He knows things.'

'Is that so?' said Vargon, turning to face him. 'I'm listening.'

'He has a great appetite for knowledge,' said Audmund. 'And clearly took a great risk in coming here alone.'

'That makes him either brave or stupid, or both,' said Vargon. 'But maybe we should talk to him anyway. See to it. Perhaps Zora will have a new pet, after all.'

The conversation made Bodric shudder. The eagle

was an impressive bird, and he was far more handsome than a buzzard could ever be. He was also very intelligent, not in the way Bodric was smart, but in a more educated way. If Zora chose Gildevard instead of him, what would his future hold?

Ripley heard the whole conversation from behind the door. Would Gildevard rat him out too? He scampered down the corridor towards the dungeon.

Chapter Eleven

A STARTLING DISCOVERY

There was a great welcome home for Timber, but the residents quickly quietened down when they saw that Jemima and Teddy weren't with him.

'We're going back for them as soon as the locket is ready,' said Timber. 'We'll need more than two minutes the next time.'

'Are they all right?' asked Dougal.

'Yes,' said Timber. 'Teddy was impatient and Jemima was bored. I just hope Vargon won't punish them because I was rescued.'

'Oh dear,' said Ramona. 'He wouldn't, would he?'

No one wanted to dwell on that, so the animals and birds huddled closer together, bracing themselves against a cold wind while Timber told the story from the beginning. The children watched them from the fairy house.

'I'd like more of you to come on the next rescue,' said Timber. 'And before we came home, I asked Queen Wanda if some of the dwarfs could help out too.'

'You mean Bushfire and Jugjaw?' said Trigger.

'Yes, and as many volunteers as they can find,' said Timber.

'That's good,' said Dougal. 'Is the shunting safe for dwarfs?'

'I asked that question too,' said Timber. 'The queen said that the dwarfs aren't like the wizards and witches. They'll be fine, just like us.' Timber looked around at all the worried faces. Although he didn't want to worry them unnecessarily, he wanted to tell them the truth. 'Zora has promised to destroy the Wandeleis and make herself queen. She sounded very angry in the manor and will stop at nothing to get what she wants. If anyone would prefer to stay here, or move away somewhere safer, I'll understand.' Everyone poo-pooed the idea. 'And there's something else.' The chatter died down. 'There's a portal somewhere in this garden and that could bring even more trouble.'

Thaddeus arrived back from Hollow Hill and went into the kitchen. Esther's spicy stew was bubbling away on the stove. The tasty smells, along with some very special ingredients, and an enormous apple pie, finally tempted the children to come to the table. While they ate, Thaddeus explained that the DimLock would be ready in the morning. He also told them about the dwarfs. 'Their magic is a little different,' he said, 'but it has been tied to ours ever since they pledged their loyalty to the queen, and as you know, our magic is rather unpredictable at the moment.'

'You mean the dwarfs' magic is a bit wonky too,' said Abigail.

'Yes, it is, but they like to use pickaxes and hammers as well as wands, useful weapons while the magic is wonky. As well as being brave, the dwarfs are good at diverting attention and generally causing mayhem. They'll be a help to you. I'm sure of it.'

'And the portal?' said Luke.

'They're immune to portals, just like goblins,' said Esther.

'Goblins?' muttered Luke. But there was no further talk of goblins.

'They'll be expecting us to go back, won't they?' asked Jamie.

'Very likely,' said Thaddeus. 'But don't worry. The queen and the dwarfs are drawing up a plan. Tomorrow, we will have Jemima and Teddy back.'

Audmund was working in his study when he heard Vargon calling him. He bundled his books and papers into a drawer, just before the angry warlock lord barged in.

'You were calling me, My Lord?'

'Why didn't you reply?' said Vargon, his large frame filling the doorway. 'I want the protection on those two prisoners trebled, not doubled. See to it, and reinforce the doors and portal too. It is laughable to think we allowed that dog to escape!' He turned to go, then stopped. 'Have you made that new potion for Zora?'

'It is not quite ready, My Lord.'

'Then get it ready! NOW!' Vargon slammed the door behind him. It shuddered and groaned, then automatically locked with a spell.

Audmund hurried to a corner of the room where there was a small stove, a stack of bottles, vials, pots and an array of ingredients for Zora's Restoration potion. He had forgotten to make a new batch, and the Youth potion too. He had been devoting all his time to other matters. Mixing the brew quickly, he set it to a strong bubble and then returned to his desk. 'Drat!' he cried, slapping his hands on his desk. 'Why can't Vargon look after those Protection charms himself?' He went over to the stove, reduced the potion to a simmer, put the pages into his secret pocket and left the study.

The augurer passed a few warlocks on his way to the dungeon. They looked bored with guard duty. He turned the corner and saw a few more. They were betting on two rats running down the corridor. 'Wait a minute,' he thought. 'They're meant to be guarding the prisoners. This is a waste of my time.'

He turned the other way and went outside. Gildevard was performing another flight display for Zora, which momentarily distracted the augurer. He quickly threw a Blocking charm over the portal. In his haste, however, he didn't notice that he hadn't covered all five pillars. Muttering to himself, he hurried back to his study, but once again something slipped his busy mind. He had forgotten to place a stronger Protection charm on the back door.

Jemima was frustrated and wished she had something to do. She could hear Teddy in the next cell, meowing and scratching at the door. They were both glad Timber had been rescued, but Jemima couldn't help wondering what was going on back in Grindlewood and whether a rescue party was really on its way.

Luckily, her ankle was feeling quite good. She didn't think she needed the crutches anymore, but she had to keep them close while the wand was hidden inside. She sighed. If only she could do magic, she would escape from her cell, free Teddy and the two of them would sneak out, and then what? Where exactly was Mord Manor?

Breakfast was the same as the previous day. The guards arrived, opened the cell door, put a bowl on the floor and then used a spell to slide it into the cell. They were taking bets to see who could slide it without spilling it. For Jemima, it was another tasteless bowl of gruel, but she usually ate it anyway, as there wouldn't be anything else for another eight hours. Poor Teddy was only thrown a lump of rotten rat through the window of his door once a day. He chewed on it slowly, only because he was so hungry.

This morning, however, Jemima didn't touch her breakfast. After the guards delivered it, she stood up and looked out the barred window to make sure they were gone. She stood behind the door and pulled the wand out of its hiding place. With a little bit of concentration, she could remember every spell Abigail had ever shown her. She pointed her wand at the tray.

'Reversum centirum!' she whispered. Nothing happened. She checked the corridor again. 'Reversum centirum!' she said in a louder voice. The tray wobbled about an inch towards the door. 'Huh?' Jemima straightened up, pointed the wand and repeated the spell in a very determined voice this time. 'Reversum centirum!' The bowl slid all the way over to the door and stopped at her feet, exactly where the guard had placed it. 'I can do it!' she gasped. 'Somehow, I can do magic!' She peered outside the cell again. The corridors were still empty. 'Whew! I must calm down before it's too late. Ready, steady

...' Taking a deep breath, she pointed the wand at the lock on the door. 'Reversum centirum!'

The lock clicked open.

Chapter Twelve

DARK SECRETS

Esther and Thaddeus sat talking in the kitchen. It was late.

'How can we let the children go on such a petrifying quest?' asked Esther.

'The queen has to make difficult decisions,' said Thaddeus. 'And Abigail cannot escape her destiny, neither can the others, especially Timber.'

'But are we sure the prophecy is real?' asked Esther. 'And what proof do we have that the orb still exists? No one has been able to find it in centuries.'

'Your sister thinks she may be able to find it,' said Thaddeus. 'More than that I cannot say.'

Esther looked surprised.

'Our biggest secret yet,' said Thaddeus, nodding. 'We must stay calm and strong for the children's sake.

I am just as concerned as you about what they are facing, but what else can be done?'

Esther didn't reply. All she could think was, 'What if it all goes horribly wrong?'

Next morning, Jugjaw and Bushfire were at the reception chamber to meet the children, dogs, Cindy – who was so concerned for Teddy that she insisted on joining them – Oberon, Thaddeus and Esther.

'Hi ho,' said one.

'Howdy,' said the other.

'Hello, Jugjaw, Bushfire,' said Thaddeus. 'Thank you for joining the rescue party.'

'You're welcome, Professor Allnutt, but it's not just us,' said Jugjaw.

'We have two dozen volunteers ready to do battle!' said Bushfire proudly.

'And Timber asked especially for us,' said Jugjaw, looking just as proud as his brother. Timber trotted over and gave them both a generous lick.

They entered the queen's outer chamber. The other dwarfs were already there, all lined up in a perfect square. Some of them carried shovels and pickaxes; all of them had wands and hammers.

'Good morning, everyone,' said Wanda. 'I am very

grateful that you offered to help the Grindlewood Army on this mission. Look out for one another and come back safe and sound. Good luck.' The queen turned to the children and Timber. 'I know you will be anxious to bring Jemima and Teddy back to safety, but I must ask you to try to find the keys and the pages too. You may not get another chance to return to the manor.'

Every time the warlocks delivered her food, Jemima practised the Reversing spell as soon as it was safe to do so. It worked every time and she was able to lock the door again by reversing the Reversing spell. 'This is so cool,' she thought. 'No wonder Mr Allnutt taught Abigail this spell. Now, maybe I could take a quick look around.' The temptation proved to be too much. She tried it on Teddy's cell. The door swung open and Teddy dashed out, delighted. 'We only have a couple of minutes, Teddy.'

Teddy skidded to a halt as Jemima tried to explain.

'I can't be sure how long the magic will last, and the wand might stop working. Then what? We really don't know where we are. If we're caught, we'll be in more trouble than we've ever known. Stay close to me.'

They crept down the corridor, looking ahead and behind, terrified that a guard would appear. They froze mid-step whenever they heard footsteps or voices in the distance, but luckily no one came their way. Then there was a loud bang. Both of them jumped. Jemima grabbed Teddy's collar, turned him around and they both headed back the way they came. 'We'll try again after supper.'

Teddy purred and rubbed the bandage on Jemima's ankle.

'Yes, it's much better, you clever cat, but we mustn't let the warlocks know.' Jemima kissed him on the head and put him back in his cell, locked it and went back to her own.

Their second attempt to sneak out was spoiled, however. The warlocks were hanging around the corridors long after supper and by the time they left the dungeon, too much time had passed to do the Reversing spell. Then Jemima had an idea. She banged on the bars of her cell window with her crutch.

A big burly warlock thundered down the corridor. 'What do you want?' he roared.

'Please, I need another glass of water. I spilled the last one and I feel really sick. My ankle is hurting and, and …' Jemima put on a crying face.

'All right, stop whinging,' roared the warlock and he marched off to fetch the drink. He returned with the glass of water, then hurried away to avoid hearing any more whining. As soon as he was gone, Jemima left her cell and then let Teddy out too. He trotted obediently beside her, his eyes, ears and nose taking in everything. As they headed down the corridor, Jemima's heart was thumping loudly.

Once again they heard a door slamming upstairs, but no footsteps. They continued down the corridor to a corner, then they heard a door being unlocked, opened, then locking again. Jemima ducked back and held her breath. Teddy crouched at her feet. Luckily, whoever it was went the other way. Peeking around the corner, Jemima recognised the grey-hooded figure moving away from her. 'Audmund, that creep!'

The temptation proved too much yet again, and once they reached Audmund's study, Jemima didn't hesitate. 'Reversum centirum!' In they went, but they weren't alone. Ripley ran in after them. 'You found Audmund's study,' he said to Teddy. The cat got an awful fright. With no scent and silent paws, Ripley could get very close before being detected. 'Listen, Teddy, I need to talk to you. I have ...'

'Not now, Ripley, we're busy and we don't have much time,' said Teddy.

'If you make a sound, I'll zap you with my wand,' said Jemima, poking her wand at the squirrel.

Ripley stared at her, then started fidgeting nervously, but he wasn't about to give them away. He watched them search around the room.

 Jemima went straight for the drawers, while Teddy sniffed through the piles of paperwork on top of the desk, then some books and papers stacked on the floor. Boxes, jars and vials seemed to take up nearly all the shelf space. Pots of red potion were still simmering on the stove.

Jemima opened a tall cupboard and saw a little box with an ornate clasp. She took it down and tried to open it. It didn't budge. 'Abigail used a spell to open the drawer in my dresser once. Accessio, no, no, that's not it. Um, Accessitus articus!' It didn't work. 'Of course not. Silly me,' she whispered. 'Audmund was bound to use some sophisticated spell, but if he only

~ 133 ~

closed it a moment ago … Reversum centirum!'

The clasp opened. Jemima gasped. 'This must be a powerful spell!'

Ripley stretched his neck to try to get a better view. Teddy looked over from where he was sniffing around on top of Audmund's desk.

'The silver key,' said Jemima, staring at it. Teddy meowed at her and waved a paw in the air. He wanted her to take it.

'That's one of the keys, Teddy,' said Ripley. 'Take it! Take it!'

Jemima had already made up her mind. She took out the key, shut the box with the Reversing spell and returned it to the shelf. Teddy was rummaging through another mound of papers. Jemima went to take a look. Peeking out from under the pile were the missing pages from *The Book of Potions and Spells*. They were unmistakeable. 'Well done, Teddy. You found them! The other ones could be here too, but we've run out of time.'

Teddy jumped down lightly from the desk, careful not to disturb anything else. Jemima quickly tidied the rest and they left.

'Run!' cried Ripley. 'Don't waste time locking the

door – it locks itself. RUN!' and he ran off himself in the opposite direction. Teddy pelted down the corridors towards their cells. Jemima raced after him. She did the Reversing spell on the cell locks just in the nick of time.

Jemima had to think quickly. Where would she hide the pages and the key? She looked around – useless, empty cell. She looked at the crutches – nope. Suddenly, she knew what to do. Sitting on the floor, she unwrapped the bandage on her ankle, down to the layer against her skin. After smoothing out the pages, she wrapped them carefully around her ankle and then wrapped the bandage on top, round and round covering the pages completely. She tucked the silver key behind her ankle bone so it wouldn't be noticeable. Luckily it was fairly small, so it wouldn't be too uncomfortable. Then she wrapped the last bit of the bandage around to the end, tucking it in tightly. 'Whew!' she thought and lay down on the mat to rest.

Teddy spent hours prowling up and down his cell, far too excited to sleep. Jemima didn't sleep much either. She was trying to figure out how she had made the spells work. On the one hand, she didn't care, she was thrilled. On the other, it was weird. Why and how had the magic worked for her?

She heard scratching next door. She peeped out and saw the tip of Ripley's tail. 'He's very keen,' she thought. 'I wonder what he's really up to.'

Teddy went to his door and sniffed along the floor in case it was something else. No scent. He listened. More scratching. It had to be the squirrel.

'What is it, Ripley?'

'Things are really bad here,' said the nervous squirrel. 'Zora is completely crazy, Lord Vargon hates me, and the eagle has it in for me. Can you get me out of here?'

'I'm the one in the cell, silly!' said Teddy. 'Wait, what eagle?'

'Gildevard, of course. But you got out, Teddy, and Jemima can do magic. There's no one else who can help me.'

Silence.

'What can we do locked up like this?' asked Teddy, still suspicious. 'We can get out of the cells but not out of the manor. How do we escape, exactly?'

'You can't risk it yet,' said Ripley. 'But promise you'll take me with you when you're rescued.'

'Rescued?'

'I've been to the garden, I know they're planning something.'

Teddy was glad to hear of a rescue, but was this a trap?

'If you've been to the garden, why didn't you just stay there, or run away like you usually do?'

'I've got this shunt stone around my neck,' said Ripley. 'If I don't return from spying, they'll come after me – Vargon, Audmund, all of them.'

'You could have asked my friends for help much sooner,' said Teddy.

'I was afraid they'd gang up on me, especially the foxes. They hate me,' said Ripley. 'But if I help you find the gold key, I would deserve some reward, wouldn't I?'

'That's for Timber to decide.'

'Um, OK,' said Ripley. 'Vargon has it, but you can't expect me to take him on. He wants to turn me into a fur collar!'

'Find out where it is and how we can get it, then we'll talk about a reward.'

Ripley scampered off.

※

It wasn't hard for Audmund to persuade the golden eagle to meet Zora. It was exactly what he wanted. Unfortunately for Bodric, his protests were ignored.

Gildevard sat patiently on Zora's windowsill, on her leather-strapped wrist, or on the new perches she had demanded for her bedroom and the parlour. He quite enjoyed the attention, but he had one thought in mind: 'This is my chance to learn a whole new realm of magic, Worfagon knowledge and learning. It is an opportunity I cannot miss. I could become the most learned golden eagle of all time.'

Despite his eagerness, the eagle had to play a clever game to win Zora over, and Bodric would not give up his old position of favour too easily. And there was another sticking point: Zora had her eye on Timber too.

'Timber is very like Tyrus, Lyra's old dog,' said Zora. She was sitting in the parlour with Vargon and Audmund after dinner. 'I think I met Tyrus in the forest once when I was a girl, before Lyra snatched him for herself. I think I'd like a dog like that, like Timber.'

'Would you?' muttered Vargon, half listening. He

was trying to enjoy his after-dinner potion.

'Yes, I would,' snapped Zora.

'Perhaps I could be of help,' said Gildevard. 'I know Timber well and I might be able to convince him to join us.'

'Do you really think so?' said Zora, staring into his eyes. 'I thought he was devoted to the children and that little queen.'

'I could try,' said Gildevard. 'And I should return soon or they might suspect something.'

'You want to leave already?' cried Zora.

'Of course not,' said Gildevard. 'I'm thinking of the bigger plan, just as Lord Vargon explained earlier.'

'I could always use a potion or a spell to capture him,' muttered Zora.

'You won't have time for all these pets,' said Vargon. 'Forget about him.'

'Are you still worried about the big dog, Vargon?' she teased.

'They're bound to be planning another rescue,' interrupted Gildevard. 'Ripley can't get close enough to Timber to find out what they're up to, but I could.'

'I always thought squirrels were useless little rodents,' said Zora. 'Very well, my eagle. Audmund, get me another of those shunt stones for Gildevard. He can use the portal whenever he wants.'

Audmund glanced at Vargon, who rolled his eyes and then nodded.

'Yes, Your Redness,' said Audmund. 'I'll go and get one from my study.'

Vargon drained the remainder of his potion and slammed the goblet onto the table beside him. 'Make sure you bring us some useful information, eagle, or I promise you I'll roast you for supper.'

Chapter Thirteen

SECRETS AND PLANS

Timber didn't like Gildevard's plan, nor did he believe the eagle was telling him all of it. 'You're taking a terrible risk.'

The eagle didn't respond.

'You must have been very convincing to get that shunt stone,' said Eldric.

'How do we know you're not on *their* side?' asked Norville, flexing his spines.

'Don't talk nonsense,' said Gildevard. 'Of course I'm convincing. If even one of the Worfagons suspects me, I'm done for. Anyway, this is my chance to observe and learn about the magic of a clan that is so hard to get close to. Most of them spend all their time arguing and fighting, and the learned ones prefer to live alone in weird dimensions. At least I can get in and out of Mord Manor easily now.'

'So, tell us what they're up to,' said Eldric.

The eagle glared at him, narrowing his eyes. 'I haven't earned that kind of trust yet.'

'I don't like it,' said Timber. 'You'd better not bring any trouble here.'

'Decide whether you trust me or not,' said Gildevard. 'Either way, I will be returning to the manor shortly.'

'Where's the portal?' asked Timber. He was curious to know if the eagle knew there was one in the garden.

'There's a small one suitable for animals and birds at the far side of the forest,' said the eagle. 'And another larger one for general use on the outskirts of the village.'

Timber decided to change the subject in case the eagle became suspicious. 'Did you see Jemima and Teddy while you were there?'

'No,' said the eagle. 'I have not been allowed near the dungeon.'

'I hope they're not too frightened,' said Cindy. 'Poor Teddy.'

'Teddy's very brave,' said Dougal, giving Cindy a quick ear lick. 'He tries to be like Timber.'

'And the only thing that frightens Jemima is spiders,' said Ramona.

'Let's hope she doesn't find any in the dungeon, then,' said Gildevard. He was getting bored with the conversation.

'We would like to be able to count on you,' said Timber.

'I'll see what I can do,' said the eagle. He was clearly in a huff, and he flew off without any useful information. He would have to think up something interesting to keep Vargon satisfied.

'I don't know what to make of him,' said Oberon, fluttering his feathers and walking in circles. 'He's so clever but so, so …'

'Difficult?' suggested Dougal. Oberon scowled again and pulled out a few more feathers.

'We can't rely on him,' said Eldric. 'It's too risky.'

Timber didn't make any comment. He wasn't sure whether to believe Gildevard or not either. It was possible he was telling lies to everyone, or only to the Worfagons, or maybe just to them. Timber talked for a while about the rescue mission, then the conversation returned to the portal in the garden.

'Having a portal means that anyone could come

here anytime,' said Eldric.

'That's true,' said Oberon. 'But I'm not sure many people know about it. I've never heard of it, but I did hear rumours about a strange place at the far end of the forest. That could be the other portal Gildevard mentioned.'

'Gildevard is not to be told about our portal, wherever it is, whenever we find it,' said Timber.

'Absolutely,' said the Brigadier. 'After all, he's not a permanent resident of the garden, is he?'

Audmund had been working on a special project. Keeping it secret from everyone, especially Vargon, had been nerve-racking. He had never done this spell before. In fact, he wasn't sure if anyone had, certainly not in his long lifetime. It had seemed like a bold and clever idea, but now, as the beads of sweat ran down his neck, his stomach churned and his hands trembled, he wasn't as sure.

Audmund had never been much of an augurer. Most of the time he had just agreed with the others; he had never had any real visions himself. But he was good at faking it, and being an augurer had given him access to information and privileges that were useful. He realised now more than ever that using magic from *The Book of Darkness* was both dangerous and complicated, and bringing someone back from the dead was riddled with risks. He had to be extremely careful. Once he took the next step, there would be no going back. He left his study and joined Vargon and Zora in the parlour.

Grizzle was roaring out in the yard. He had been stuck there for ages and was bored out of his mind. The soothing potions were having less and less effect.

'Can't you keep that ugly mutt quiet?' Vargon yelled as soon as Audmund entered the room.

'I could move him to my study,' said Audmund, thinking Grizzle might deter any intruders, even Vargon.

'A walloping beast like that? Absolutely not!' Vargon eyed him suspiciously. 'I'd like to know what's going on in that study of yours, Audmund. Perhaps I will surprise you with a visit.'

'Any time, My Lord.'

'Dwarf-troll,' said Zora. 'Grizzle. Even the words are revolting.'

'Buzzards aren't known for their good looks either, Your Redness,' said Audmund.

Both Bodric and Zora glared at him. Bodric skulked away quietly.

'Indeed,' said Zora. 'But I have a handsome pet now, quite the perfect companion for a powerful queen.'

Vargon sighed. He was becoming increasingly irritated by Zora, and worried too. As her strength slowly returned, her impatience increased. He feared she might leave the manor again and mess things up even more. With little else to do but try on dresses and take potions, Zora had plenty of time to concoct reckless plans.

'In all the time I was away, why didn't anyone use a Destroyer spell on Hollow Hill?' she asked. 'I thought you would have done it for me, Vargon, although I'm glad now that you didn't, because I intend to.'

'Not until I say so,' said Vargon. 'We are *all* going to stick to *my plan*.'

'It had better be worth all this tip-toeing around,'

said Zora. 'When are we going to make our move?'

'Soon,' said Vargon. 'I'm working on a nasty surprise.'

'And what are you working on, Audmund?' asked Zora.

'Whatever I am asked, Your Redness,' said Audmund. He didn't want to be asked any more questions, so he made an excuse and left the parlour. Zora grew tired of bickering with Vargon and went to her room to try on some new gowns.

Vargon could sense they were both up to something and it annoyed him.

The two prisoners were managing to explore a bit more of the manor, thanks to Jemima's night-time requests for water, and a very daring idea. She had been listening carefully to the warlocks' jabbering ever since their arrival and in particular the words they used to cast spells. If a Wandelei spell worked for her, why not a Worfagon spell?

She practised saying the clunky Worfagon words every time the guards were out of earshot. They sometimes used a complicated old dialect that was difficult to pronounce. Strangely, they used the same spell to both lock and unlock the cell doors. Once Jemima felt she had mastered it, she put it to the test. No luck. She wasn't surprised though; it was unlikely that a Worfagon spell would work without also using a Worfagon wand.

On their way back from another two-minute look around, Jemima and Teddy were dismayed to find they had to slip past a sleeping warlock. They heard his snoring and smelled his hideous odour before they turned the corner and saw him. Without a hint of nerves, Teddy headed straight for the snoring guard. But instead of passing by, he stopped and pawed gently at the warlock's wand. It fell to the ground with an unfortunate clatter. Jemima froze mid-step and Teddy's fur stood on end. Somehow the warlock didn't wake. He snuffled and stirred in his chair, then continued to snore. Jemima crept forward, holding her breath as she picked up the wand. Then they hurried back to their cells. No one would suspect that the prisoners had taken the wand!

A couple of hours later, when the guard had moved off, Jemima decided to try it out. She rehearsed the word in her head a few more times, then gave it her best shot: 'Klink-klutterall-klankentum!'

It worked.

They explored the other corridors in the dungeon, for longer this time. They went upstairs too, once to listen outside the parlour and once to the kitchen, where they managed to steal a piece of cake for Jemima and a lump of tuna for Teddy – tasty morsels after all the horrid slop.

They tried all of the outer doors and windows but they were locked with different spells. None of them responded to any of Jemima's attempts. She paused to look out one of the many long and grubby windows of an outer corridor, hoping to get a sense of where they were. Although it was dark, Jemima could see movement in the trees outside – large, lumbering shapes shifting from side to side. Perhaps it was a trick of the light. Perhaps not. 'It's as creepy outside as it is in here,' she thought. She looked around for Teddy. No sign.

The curious cat had wandered down another corridor, a narrower one that they hadn't noticed before. He stopped to sniff outside a door, when suddenly Vargon burst out and Teddy was thrown out of sight. Luckily, Vargon hurried away without looking behind him. Teddy took his chance and darted into Vargon's study. The door closed loudly and ominously behind him, locking with a spell.

Jemima was still looking for Teddy when she heard the guards' heavy footsteps. There was no choice but to hurry back to her cell, leaving Teddy somewhere out there. She locked the doors with her wand. 'It isn't food time. What are they doing?' she thought. They passed by without stopping. A minute later the squirrel was scratching at the door. After checking to see that no one was with him, Jemima went quietly out. Ripley beckoned her to follow.

Teddy decided he might as well look around Vargon's study while he waited and hoped that Jemima would find him. There was something eerie about the dark, shadowy room. He saw vials full of thick black liquid and a range of jars that contained eyeballs, claws, dead beetles, rotting worms and giant centipedes. They were all labelled in witch language and arranged neatly on shelves, largest to smallest, left to right. There was a pot of brown, bubbling goo sitting on a table. Empty bottles sat beside it, waiting to be filled. A big furry spider was angrily trying to get out of a glass box. Teddy hissed at him and to his surprise, the spider hissed back. A box on the shelf just above the spider caught his eye. 'That might hold the gold key,' he thought, but his thoughts were rudely interrupted.

Vargon flung the door open and limped in, thumping his stick into the carpet. 'That ungrateful little brat!' he cried. 'After all I've done for her, she gives me nothing but headaches and backaches, and my leg hurts!' He threw his stick on the floor, poured himself a drink of something lumpy and purple and then slumped into an armchair. He drank the potion in three big gulps and soon dozed off.

Teddy peeked out from his hiding place, a big fur coat that was lying on another chair. His eyes darted around the room. He couldn't see a way out. Time ticked by. Teddy had to think what he would do once Vargon woke up. To his horror, he heard Zora's boots click-clacking along the corridor. She hammered on the door, waking the old tutor with a start. He opened it with a wave of his wand.

'Is my Youth potion ready?' asked Zora.

'I have made the serum for you,' said Vargon. 'Audmund is preparing the potion. Once you start this treatment, you'll have to keep taking it or you'll age even faster.' He handed her a small yellow vial. 'One drop a day, Zora. Only one.'

'This had better work,' Zora snapped. 'I want my looks back as well as everything else I lost.' She whirled out of the room and the door locked behind her. Vargon picked up a few papers from the table beside him, then he tossed them away. He couldn't concentrate or relax. Too many things were bothering him. He poured another goblet of the purple stuff and drank it quickly. He settled back into the armchair, tucking a rug around his legs. This time he fell into a deep sleep.

Ripley had spotted where Teddy had gone and he led Jemima to Vargon's door. He kept nodding to her and pointing to the wands, her own and the warlock's. Jemima was terrified it was a trick. She couldn't be sure what was behind the door, but something told her it must be Teddy, and if he was discovered, Vargon would surely kill him.

She raised both wands and said both spells,

'Reversum centirum! Klink-klutterall-klankentum!'

The door swung gently open without a sound. 'Wow!' she thought. 'I opened Vargon's study!' Teddy ran out, Jemima gently pulled the door shut, and they hurried away.

'Did you get the key?' Ripley asked Teddy, as Jemima bundled the cat into his cell.

'No,' said Teddy. 'Vargon was in there.'

'Ooooh!' said Ripley, withering at the thought. 'How did you … Oooh!'

'I was lucky,' said Teddy. 'We'll try again later.'

Jemima locked Teddy's cell door. 'Thanks for showing me where Teddy was,' she whispered to Ripley. Then she went into her own cell and locked her door too. Ripley ran off.

Later that night, Vargon woke from a dreadful nightmare. He mopped his brow and drank another potion, then left his study and headed towards the dungeon. He stood in a corridor, waved his wand in the air and then waited. He didn't like the answer. He did the same in the next corridor, and the next and the next. 'That fool Audmund didn't do what I asked,' he said to the night. He waved his wand outside each of the cells in the dungeon, doubling and redoubling the protection on the locks. Then he headed off to bed, mumbling and grumbling to himself.

Jemima tried all the spells she knew as soon as Vargon was out of sight. None of them worked. 'We've run out of luck,' she said to herself. 'Now we'll just have to wait for the rescue.'

Chapter Fourteen

INTO MORD MANOR

It was just after supper when word came from Hollow Hill that the queen wanted to see the children, Timber, the dwarfs and the professors.

'The DimLock is ready,' she said. 'You will be leaving at midnight.'

'Midnight?' said Jamie. 'But you said it's ready.'

'It is,' said Wanda. 'But tonight's full moon will help keep the portal stable, and there will be quite a few of you travelling through it.'

'The sun and the moon are very important in our magic,' said Pendrick.

'Are we going from the garden?' asked Abigail.

'No, I want you to use another portal, at the end of the village,' said the queen.

'There's a tunnel that will take us close to it,' said Thaddeus.

'When you reach the manor, two of the dwarfs will remain at the portal to keep it open,' said Pendrick. 'If you need to leave quickly, there won't be time for any chant.'

Timber told the queen he wanted the dogs, cat, fox and owl to go too. He also told her about his conversation with Gildevard.

'You may take as many of your garden friends as you need,' said the queen, speaking to all of them. 'As for the eagle, he may be both your friend and your enemy, so be careful.'

They returned home and got everything ready. It felt like a long, long time, waiting to go on the quest. When it was finally time to leave, Timber went to the back door of the main house and sat there, waiting to be let in. They had forgotten something.

'What does he want?' asked Luke.

'I don't know but it must be important,' said Jamie, as he let the dog in and followed him upstairs. Timber pawed and nosed at the bottom drawer of the dresser in the corner of Jemima's bedroom. Jamie opened the drawer, suddenly remembering what his sister had hidden there. 'Good boy, Timber!' He took the pouch and ran down to the others.

'How could we have forgotten the gems?' asked Luke. 'We need all the magic we can get.'

'I'll take them,' said Abigail. 'You two have enough to carry.' She took the pouch and zipped it inside her coat pocket. Her wand was hidden in a specially designed pocket down the side of her coat. The boys checked their stuff: Jamie's wooden sword that would turn into steel, and Gorlan's ring, which he placed on his finger; Luke's bow and double quiver of arrows, which he slung over his shoulder. They were all set.

Trigger, Dougal, Cindy, Eldric and Oberon stood around Timber as he pointed his nose in the air and prepared to howl loudly. The whole of the garden knew what it meant: this would be a big test.

'We each know what to do,' said Timber when he finished. They nodded back at him. He turned to the other animals and birds. 'Take care of the garden and remember, trouble might strike at any time and in any disguise. Keep watch in the forest too. Good luck, everyone.'

They all wished each other well as Timber turned to Jamie. He barked and scraped his paws on the ground.

'They're ready,' said Jamie, petting his dog.

'And it's just midnight,' said Luke. 'Wait! Shouldn't we bring Ernie?'

Timber shook his ears and pawed at the ground again. The queen had told him that the frog's magic wouldn't work in Vargon's dimension.

'I think Timber is saying no,' said Jamie. 'Hang on.' He went over to the Brigadier. 'Brig, make sure Ernie is ready to meet us when we get back, OK?' The beagle barked and wagged his tail, and Timber barked his 'yes' bark. It was likely some of them would need Ernie's healing powers, once they returned. They set off down the trap door. Thaddeus, Sparks and the dwarfs met them at the crossroads in the tunnels.

'I hope this portal is well hidden,' said Luke, 'or they'll need an awful lot of memory mist to make the locals forget it.'

'Don't worry,' said Thaddeus. 'It's tucked away behind some trees and it's late. No one should see us, and a few of my friends will be on hand just in case.'

They walked along without much chat, listening to the dwarfs sing an old battle song.

'Hum de ho, hum de ho, into battle we all go.'

It went on and on with very few other words.

'Bodric and Ripley may turn up,' said Timber. 'And if Audmund is there, Grizzle might be too.'

'And possibly the hawks,' said Oberon. 'But I hope there aren't any new surprises.'

Even using the tunnel, it was still a long walk to the end of the village. They emerged in a copse at the edge of a field.

'In here, everyone,' said Thaddeus. Instead of a stone, there was an old urn in the middle of a circle of birch trees. It was covered with symbols.

'Abigail, the queen asked that you wear the DimLock,' said Sparks. He put the gold chain over her head. 'This time, close and twist the top half of the locket when it's time to return, and not a second before.'

'Stand close together,' said Thaddeus. 'A dozen dwarfs first, then the children and pets, then the remaining dwarfs at the rear.' Everyone got into place. 'When Sparks says go, walk quickly through the ring of light. Understood?'

'Yes, sir, understood,' said Bushfire. The children nodded, the pets shook their ears or feathers and the rest of the dwarfs gave a thumbs-up. Thaddeus and

Pendrick began the chant. The blue ring of light appeared and hovered over the stone, pulsing brightly.

'GO!' cried Sparks. The blue light popped as soon as the last dwarf passed through.

Thaddeus looked at Sparks. 'And now we wait.'

⁂

They arrived outside the wall that surrounded Mord Manor. It was dark, though not night-time, and it was cold and quiet.

'Have we lost hours again?' asked Luke.

'Nah!' said Jugjaw. 'It's always gloomy in these Worfagon dumps!'

'Look at the moon,' whispered Abigail. It was a deep shade of red.

'Creepy,' said Jamie.

'Get ready,' said Bushfire. 'They'll soon realise that someone came through their portal.'

Two dwarfs remained at the portal and two more stayed on guard close by, in case anything happened to the first pair. The rest broke into smaller groups and they crept towards the front and sides of the manor, staying hidden as best they could. There was a scattering of thorny bushes and the odd spindly tree, as well as several ruins of statues and sculptures strewn about the courtyard. Most provided somewhere to hide. Timber asked Oberon to circle the manor. He reported back quickly. 'I saw a woman dressed in red in a red room at the back of the manor, which is also streaked red,' said the owl as he landed. 'Zora, I assume. Gildevard is perched beside her, looking quite the show-off.'

'What on earth is he up to?' said Timber crossly.

'They know we're here,' cried Bushfire. 'Look sharp!'

Around fifty warlocks roared and hollered as they charged out from their quarters behind the manor. More spilled out the front and side doors of the house itself. They looked fierce in their clunky armour, brandishing heavy swords and spiked clubs.

The dwarfs turned to face them bravely, though they were less than half their size. Some dwarfs fired repeating spells, dozens and dozens of them, though not all of them worked very well. The dwarf magic was not only unreliable, but in this dimension, quite explosive too. Others ran and jumped at the warlocks, swinging their hammers in rapid circles, then releasing them to fly out and knock their target down. The newly sharpened pickaxes inflicted nasty wounds on arms and legs, as the nimble dwarfs scurried around the clumsy, heavy warriors.

Timber led the animals in one tight pack. They closed in on one warlock after another, pulling or knocking them to the ground. Then the dwarfs rushed in and knocked them out completely with a hammer or an axe.

Abigail fired her new Numbing spells that she had practised that afternoon. Luke used his bow; his long practice sessions with Jamie had increased his confidence and skill. Jamie's wooden sword turned willingly to steel as Gorlan's ring flashed brightly on his finger. He attacked several warlocks, destroying their wands by chopping them in half, reducing any threat of enemy spells.

Overall the warlocks were doing rather badly. They were disorganised and awkward, clearly surprised by their intruders, and their tempers were rising. After a while, however, they made some changes to their tactics. A few warlocks went up to the roof and fired rocks and clubs down onto the courtyard. The dwarfs responded by throwing their hammers skyward to knock them out. Luke fired arrows towards the roof and Abigail cast spells in their direction too. Several of the warlocks were so numbed, jellied or simply annoyed, that they toppled over the parapet and plunged to the ground.

'LOOK OUT!' cried Bushfire, as another warlock crashed into the yard, taking out a few others where he fell. So far, it was going according to plan.

Chapter Fifteen

SECOND RESCUE

Oberon and Bodric almost clashed near the portal, but the buzzard sensibly retreated. He hid in a thorny bush and used the Mind-meld to contact Zora. He had a daring suggestion – that the eagle should prove his loyalty and deal with the snowy owl.

'Excellent idea!' said Zora when she received the message. 'I'd love to see my eagle display his fighting skills.'

Vargon, Zora and Audmund stood on a balcony overlooking the front courtyard, watching the spectacle unfold. Audmund was largely hidden by his voluminous cloak and deep hood. Zora looked a little perkier having just taken another potion. Vargon, however, looked ill. His face was deeply lined and his skin had a greyish tinge to it.

'This was totally unnecessary,' he said. 'A complete waste of our time.'

'The warlocks were getting bored, My Lord,' said Audmund. 'No harm in a little exercise and entertainment.'

'Worfagon warlocks against a bunch of dwarfs, three children and their pets,' said Zora. 'Is that what entertains you, Audmund?' She stroked the eagle's feathers as he sat on her gauntlet. 'Off you go now, Gildevard. Tear that fluffy owl apart.'

The golden eagle flew out over the mayhem below. Somehow, he would have to make it look like he had killed the owl, and the owl would have to cooperate, otherwise they were both in trouble. He bowed to Zora, keeping his face as blank as ever. He circled a few times, screeching to impress her, then he gave the owl a warning cry. Oberon heard him and flew into a cluster of tall trees, where they could remain out of sight for a few minutes.

'What about letting Grizzle have some fun as well?' said Audmund. 'A bit of fighting might do him good, and after all, he's met these do-gooders before.'

'That lumpy numbskull!' said Vargon. 'Didn't he almost lose his eye the last time?' Vargon had a sudden fit of coughing.

'A minor detail,' said Audmund. 'I think you might be pleasantly surprised.'

'All right,' roared Vargon. 'Let's see if your beast can entertain me.' He turned to the warlocks standing on guard behind them. 'Release the dwarf-troll!' After another bout of wheezing and coughing, he turned to the guards again. 'Release my bats as well, and then bring me some of my Worm potion from the kitchen.'

The guards bowed. Audmund followed them downstairs and out to the back yard. Grizzle was so incensed he nearly punched the guards as they tried to unchain him. Audmund jumped out of the way as Grizzle let out a mighty roar and thundered around the side of the manor. He swatted away a couple of dwarfs and warlocks, not really caring who was who, and he continued barging and bashing his way around till he had almost reached the courtyard. Audmund rolled his eyes with frustration, and headed back inside.

Up in a tall tree, the birds of prey were arguing.

'What are you playing at?' asked Oberon crossly.

'Be careful,' said the eagle. 'I've been instructed to kill you.'

'Is that some sort of joke?' asked the owl. 'Can't you see what's going on down there?'

'Let's flutter about in here for a moment and *pretend* we're fighting,' said Gildevard. 'We can talk at the same time.'

The children and pets had moved nearer the portal to deal with a cluster of warlocks who suddenly charged at the dwarfs who were on guard. Jamie and Luke ran to the rescue with sword and arrows. Abigail was nearby casting spells as fast as she could. Bushfire and Jugjaw stayed close to the children at first, deflecting any Worfagon spells that were aimed at the children, though their wands were buckled and smoking.

The warlocks were tiring quickly in their heavy, clumsy armour and were often outmanoeuvred by the nimbler dwarfs, the even more agile animals and the very determined children. Soon most of the Worfagons were either injured, frozen, jellied, fed up or exhausted. Grizzle was still bashing them out of frustration, even though he was meant to be on their side.

Timber howled – it was time to find Jemima and

Teddy. He barked orders to the dwarfs and animals to reorganise themselves for the big rescue.

'Timber's giving instructions,' cried Jamie. 'Come on.'

'I thought there would be a lot more warlocks,' said Abigail, hurrying after the boys. 'And why are those two watching us from the balcony?'

'Two? Where's Audmund?' asked Jamie.

'I saw him leave the balcony,' said Luke. 'But he could turn up anywhere, and there could be more warlocks on the way. We should hurry.'

Timber continued barking as he ran to the side of the building.

'Follow Timber,' cried Jamie. 'He knows where to go.'

Jugjaw and Bushfire and a small group of dwarfs ran after the children and the animals. The rest were spread out around the courtyard. Some watched the front door, others the portal, while a few more patrolled the area, checking to see if any warlocks were coming out of the spells. There were only a few Worfagons still battling.

Timber figured that the back door was the closest entrance to the dungeon. The dwarfs tried spells first,

~ 168 ~

then they tried hammering and axing, but the big studded door wouldn't budge.

'Wait!' cried Abigail. She took out the first stone, the emerald. 'What about this?'

'Yes, do it!' cried Jamie. Luke nodded. Abigail held the stone tight, closed her eyes and wished for the door to be *always* open to them. After a heavy clunk and a couple of squeaks and clicks, it swung open.

'Quick, in!' cried Bushfire. 'Magic might not last in this place!'

'Watch out for enchantments!' cried Jugjaw.

The animals were so keen to find Teddy and Jemima, they charged after Timber as he led them down the corridor. As they turned the corner, they ran straight into another group of warlocks who were guarding the stairwell to the prisoners.

'So this is where the rest of them are hiding,' barked Timber.

The dwarfs battled first with their wands as they were hit with a barrage of spells. Abigail fired a few too, ducking back into doorways or behind pillars to avoid being hit herself. The dwarfs climbed into an elaborate formation, leaping, rolling, ducking and diving like an acrobatic team. It was their only way to really surprise their opponents as their spells were becoming so unpredictable, they often exploded in their faces. As more and more wands went on fire, they were forced to rely on their hammers and pickaxes too.

'I could do with a Retrieving spell for my arrows,' said Luke, shooting arrows alongside Jugjaw as the dwarf hurled his pickaxe and it flew right back to him. He flung it again, this time sending it spiralling through the air. It knocked out a tall warlock at the back, who then knocked out another beside him when he bumped him face first into a wall. The pickaxe flew straight back to its owner. 'It takes some practice to catch it, you know,' said Jugjaw. He smiled a wide, jagged grin.

'I'll bet,' said Luke as he dodged another spell.

Jugjaw ran off and charged at another huge warlock, whacking away at his ankles as Timber crashed into him from behind, buckling his knees. It took three more dwarfs to finally knock him out with their hammers.

Timber repeated his knee-buckling charge again and again as he ran for the warlocks' legs, taking them down, stopping them from casting spells or throwing clubs. Then Jamie ran in to chop their weapons, Luke pinned their hands, arms or tunics with arrows and the dwarfs did the rest. Cindy and Eldric went for hands and wands, crunching the wood into pieces, or cutting the hands enough to make each warlock drop his wand. They were doing well. Then they heard Grizzle.

The dwarf-troll had finally fought his way out of the bushes, past a few warlocks and dwarfs. He had become bored with throwing lumps of broken sculpture but he was still in a frightful rage. Steam puffed from his wide nostrils as he thundered around, his newly repaired orange eye glaring mercilessly. One of his tusks had cracked and chipped after ramming a warlock into a lump of stone, fuelling his anger further. He turned to face a bunch of dwarfs who were creeping up behind him.

Vargon's flock of vampire bats flew in from the forest and headed straight for the manor. They hovered in front of the balcony where their master chanted instructions. They screeched eerily and bared their razor-like teeth before flying around the building.

Dozens flew in the back door and down the corridor. Everyone ducked as the first group flew overhead, turned and flew back again. The next group flew straight through the windows, smashing the glass and sending shards and splinters flying about.

'They're not like the ones we saw in our garden, are they?' said Jamie.

'Nope, definitely not on our side,' said Luke.

The bats continued zooming up and down the corridor, bumping against walls and doors, up and down, back and forth, screeching continuously.

'Yikes!' said Abigail. 'Be careful everyone!'

'Stay low!' cried Jamie. 'Here they come!'

They huddled in a tight group with the animals. Timber turned to Cindy and Eldric. 'You two sniff out Jemima and Teddy. GO!'

The fox and cat skirted around everyone's feet till they reached the wall and began their hunt. A few more dwarfs bundled into the corridor to help, having seen how many bats had flown inside. Bushfire gave the order to charge and the dwarfs rushed forward, their battle cries adding to the din. The three dogs were involved in close fighting as the bats swooped to attack. For a few minutes, the corridor looked like an ocean of stormy black waves.

It didn't take Cindy and Eldric long to sniff out the two prisoners in the dungeon below them. Teddy was scratching and jumping at his cell door, and Jemima was shouting and banging her crutches on the bars of the window. Cindy ran back to Timber for help, but it took a minute or two to get his attention as he was battling bats and a warlock at the same time. Timber barked for Bushfire, but he couldn't hear the dog's bark over the bats' screeching and his own roaring. Eventually Timber had to leave the warlock, run to Bushfire and jump on him, grabbing at his belt to pull him away from the fight.

'Teddy and Jemima are down that corridor, down the stairs!' he barked. 'That way.' He pointed with his nose to where Cindy was waiting to show them the way. Bushfire and Jugjaw ran to the dungeon and found Jemima and Teddy, but none of their weapons could open the doors. Jemima was trying everything from the inside, using her own wand, the warlock's wand, the two wands together and every spell she could think of. Nothing worked. Vargon had made sure of it.

'They'll have to use another stone,' cried Bushfire.

He turned and roared 'Ahhhh!' as he walloped and hammered a number of bats who had followed them and tried to surround them. Timber was already running to find Abigail. He grabbed the end of her coat with his teeth and pulled her in the direction of the cells.

'What? Have you found them?' she cried.

Timber let go of her coat, turned and bounded towards the cells. Abigail followed. When they stood outside Jemima's cell, Timber began nosing at Abigail's pocket, but she already knew what to do. She took out the next stone, the amethyst, held it tight and wished for the doors to unlock. They did – the power of Queen Lyra's gems was greater than Vargon's locking spell.

Jemima came out holding her wand in one hand and her crutches in the other. The Worfagon wand had burst into flames and lay sizzling on the floor. Teddy bolted out of his cell and followed Timber and Cindy back upstairs, straight into the fight. Jemima hugged Abigail and they ran up to the others, all the while avoiding more bats, and the occasional warlock's spell as they reached the upper floor.

'Hi, Jem, glad you're back,' cried Jamie. 'Help Luke reload!'

Luke was firing arrows extremely fast. Every bat

he hit turned to dust, but he was quickly running out of arrows.

'This didn't work earlier but it's worth another try,' said Abigail. 'Retrievo Luke!' It worked this time.

'Retrievo Luke!' repeated Jemima. It worked for her too. The arrows that were lying on the ground flew straight back to Luke's quiver. He was speechless for just a second, then he quickly focused and reloaded his bow, again and again. The girls kept bringing the arrows back to be shot again, in between firing Freezing, Numbing and Jelly spells. Now and again Jemima walloped a few bats with her crutches too. Jamie roared with delight.

'YES!' he cried, 'We're definitely winning!' and he slashed at the bats again.

'Jemima!' said Abigail. 'That's fantastic! How … I mean … how?'

'It just happened,' said Jemima, dodging a spell and then a few bats. 'It's the wand from the cellar. It works!'

The bats were slowly but steadily driven towards the outer door and outside. The children, pets and dwarfs hurried after them, stepping over fallen warlocks, and pressing towards the courtyard again. Then they saw Grizzle.

'Oh, no, not again,' said Jamie.

'Leave him to us,' said Bushfire. 'You've got other things to do.' He called to a team of dwarfs. They ran around the angry dwarf-troll, hopped onto him, hammered him, tried a few spells – mostly small explosions – and then stuck a few pickaxes in him too. Grizzle spun around angrily, lashing out with his huge fists.

'Our team isn't doing very well, Vargon,' said Zora. 'Tell me you have a better *plan* than this.'

'Kidnapping wasn't part of the plan,' said Vargon, 'but it did have consequences, as you can see.'

'Where are the rest of our warriors?' asked Zora.

'They're in other dimensions,' said Vargon, 'gathering weapons and recruits for *later*.'

'Well,' said Zora, turning to go, 'I'm sure you can take care of this mess.'

Vargon leaned over the balcony and looked down at the chaos. Grizzle let out a roar after being hit in the nose by a pickaxe. The dwarfs cheered loudly.

'Wait!' cried Vargon. 'There's something I want you to see.' He took a whistle out of his pocket and blew on it.

'Oh, a whistle,' said Zora, unimpressed.

'Look to the forest,' said Vargon.

First there was a lot of rustling and shuffling in the trees. Then there were slow, dragging movements. Something was waking up and moving steadily towards the courtyard. Smaller trees keeled over as the monsters rumbled past or straight through them. There was a clack-clack or two, then more, and more, until there was quite a clattering. Oberon and Gildevard saw them first.

'Good grief!' said the owl.

The eagle frowned. He didn't like to admit it, but he too was unnerved by what he saw coming out of the forest.

'We have to get out of here,' said the owl and turned to go. 'Aren't you coming?'

'I'll say I was distracted by that,' said the eagle. 'Go. I'll follow in a minute.'

Oberon flew off to give Timber the bad news, but the animals had already smelled the danger.

'Wheeeeew! What is that?' barked Eldric.

'Oberon, did you find Gildevard?' asked Timber.

'He's busy deciding what to do,'

said the owl as he landed. 'There's a bigger problem. A cluster of huge spiders is heading this way.'

Timber barked to the others. The dwarfs looked concerned for the first time since they'd arrived. Even the bats were leaving in a hurry.

'There's big trouble comin',' said Jugjaw, spreading the word.

'More trouble than this?' said Jamie.

'Uh, oh,' said Luke, pointing to the trees. 'Look over there.'

'On no!' shrieked Jemima. 'Not spiders!'

Chapter Sixteen

SPIDER SWARM

Everyone's heart beat a little faster when they realised what was coming. Timber barked orders to Bushfire and he passed on the command. 'Dwarfs – in formation – NOW!' he roared at his troops. The dwarfs bustled around, sorting themselves into position. They pointed any wands that weren't smouldering, and all their hammers and pickaxes, at the oncoming enemy – a spider swarm.

They were huge and black, some standing even taller than the manor's boundary wall. Their legs had long, pointed talons, some raised menacingly in the air as they shuffled towards the courtyard. Sharp bristles spiked all over their bodies, many with red tips, undoubtedly poisonous. Six hooked teeth protruded from their mouths and their eyes spun wildly in their bulbous heads.

'Crikey!' croaked Jamie.

The others were speechless as they readied themselves behind some broken statues with the pets.

'This is a bit of a surprise,' said Dougal, gulping.

'We'll attack together,' said Timber. 'Go for their legs, one spider at a time. Do not try anything alone.' The animals nodded. 'Oberon, stay above us and toot loudly if you spot anything we should know about. And stay out of their reach.' The owl nodded and took off.

Timber joined Teddy as he tried to soothe Jemima. Ramona had been right: if there was one thing that terrified her, it was spiders. The cat rubbed his face against her legs and hands, trying to reassure her. She looked petrified.

'You have a wand now,' said Abigail, trying her best to distract her friend. 'You can do real magic, just think about that.'

Jemima stared at the ground.

'Jem,' said Jamie. 'I know you've always hated spiders and I'm sorry I ever tried to scare you with them, but this is completely different.'

'Yeah, different worse,' muttered Jemima.

'No, Abi's right,' said Jamie. 'You can do magic, just

~ 180 ~

like you've always dreamed of. And we really need you to use that magic now. It's just magic against magic – it never scared you before.'

'But they're so *big*,' whispered Jemima, still staring at the ground.

'But they're not real,' said Jamie.

'And they'll turn to dust or mush or maybe vanish,' said Abigail, 'just like the bats, hawks and ferrets did. Remember?'

'I sure hope so,' whispered Jamie.

The encouragement wasn't going very well. Then it was Luke's turn.

'I don't know how you can do it,' he said. 'But magic is a privilege. It means you're special. We don't know anyone else who can do magic who isn't a witch or a wizard. Do we?'

Finally, Jemima looked up, suddenly realising that she had a big responsibility. 'You're right,' she said. 'Magic is a gift. I must use it every chance I get, even though I don't know how I can do it, or why it chose me.' Suddenly her fears melted away and the plucky, excited Jemima was back, speaking at warp speed again. 'You know, I even managed to get out of my cell a few times. And Teddy and I found the silver key,

and the pages! We were so busy with the bats, I forgot to tell you. I have them with me, they're hidden under my bandages.'

'Fantastic!' said Luke.

'Brilliant!' said Jamie. 'Get ready. Here they come!'

They peered over great lumps of broken statues as the first spider lumbered into the courtyard.

'At least they're slow,' said Luke.

'No risks, Timber, OK?' said Jamie, looking at his dog.

Timber gave him a quick lick, then turned his attention back to the spiders. They hadn't expected anything like this, but Timber had figured out what they were going to do and he had just explained his plan to the other pets.

Abigail spoke to Jemima. 'We'll cast the first spells together. Ready?'

Jemima took a deep breath, put on her most determined face and pointed her wand alongside Abigail's. Jamie raised his sword and Luke took aim with his bow. The animals were poised and ready, growling and hissing. Oberon screeched above them. Gildevard was nowhere in sight.

The dwarfs charged out at the first spider. It was

very big, but slow and awkward. The animals followed while the children dealt with some rogue bats that had suddenly returned, as well as a couple of warlocks who had woken up from earlier spells.

A host of unpredictable spells and waves of silver arrows flew around the courtyard. All the while the spiders edged closer, their taloned feet clacking ominously and loudly once they reached the paving stones of the courtyard.

Two dwarfs were reckless and went too close. They were speared by the front spider's talons. One dwarf was flung into the bushes, while the other ended up flying through the portal.

The dogs, cats and fox charged together. They tried to confuse the spider by ducking and diving underneath its big body. Aiming for one leg at a time, they tried to bite above the top of the talon, hoping to find a weak point and buckle it. It was frightfully tricky. Some of them were simply kicked out of the way, others almost got speared.

The girls concentrated on the last few bats and any warlocks that needed a second Freeze-out or Wobble spell. They had it under control so Jamie and Luke went to help the animals. The two of them rushed towards the first spider. A group of dwarfs followed quickly behind them. After a lot of slashing, hammering and axing, the spider finally fell and was completely crushed by the others that were pressing forward.

'Spider number two!' cried Bushfire. He leapt onto the side of the next spider, climbed onto its head, carefully hopping around the poisonous bristles, and with a tremendous wallop, he stuck his pickaxe into one eye. The spider squealed and tried to turn, two of its claws clacking wildly in the air. Jugjaw copied his brother and used his pickaxe to haul himself up the other side of the spider's bulging belly, then onto its back, then its head, and then he hacked at the other eye. The spider collapsed, shrieking, not caring what was happening to its legs. The boys and the animals continued hacking and biting the spider's legs and the dwarfs finished it off. Two down, but dozens more to come.

Meanwhile, the cats, dogs and fox were working on the next spider's legs. Luke and Jamie followed them and attacked with their arrows and sword. Jemima and Abigail had dealt with all the bats for the moment and most of the remaining warlocks were stuck the far side of the spider swarm and Grizzle. They tried a few Hot spells to burn off the poison-tipped bristles and melt the spiders' armoured claws.

'Caloricum totalis!' said Abigail. 'I've never even practised that one!'

The spider finally toppled over, singed, deflating and oozing green goo. Three down.

Vargon was still watching from the balcony. He recognised Jamie's magical weapon, just as Audmund had before. 'Well, well, the boy has Gorlan's ring, and so his toy sword turns into one of steel,' he thought. 'Audmund must have known. Why didn't he mention it? This invasion is his fault too! By taking the keys, he practically invited them here! Well, I have more tricks up my sleeve.' He raised his wand and began to chant.

As Luke raised his bow to take aim again, he spotted what Vargon was doing. 'Watch out!' he cried to the others.

Jamie looked up and saw Vargon waving his arms in the air. 'Everybody duck!'

The animals gathered beside the children, but some of the dwarfs got caught by the next big spider as they were trying to regroup. Four of them lay on the ground, badly injured. Everyone else was afraid to move as they waited for Vargon's spell to appear.

'Nothing happened,' said Luke.

'Never mind,' said Jamie. 'We have to get across the courtyard, find the other key and then go to the portal.'

'We have to get past that very, very big spider first,' said Jemima, staring straight at it.

Following her gaze, they all saw that the next one was truly gargantuan.

'Oh crikey!' said Jamie. 'Right. Everyone ready?' Timber barked but he didn't wait. He charged out, the other animals close behind him. Jamie tore after them.

'Hey, you're meant to stick with us!' cried Bushfire. Then he too hurried into the fray, followed by a few dwarfs.

Jemima, Abigail and Luke continued firing at the same spider that Jamie and the animals were attacking, but all of them were worried. This particular spider was bigger, faster and smarter too.

'That one has learned from the others,' said Luke. 'It's going to be harder to stop.'

'Vargon's done something to it,' said Abigail.

Timber buckled one of the spider's legs with

repeated bites. Jamie stabbed with his sword at another one. They were sure of the weak spot now, just above the hard shell of the talon. The spider screeched and a second leg went down. The other animals quickly attacked a third leg and then another. The spider kicked at them and tried to turn but its heavy body was teetering on fewer legs, and the other spiders were pressing strongly behind. The was very little room for anyone to move.

As the spider slowly fell to one side, Jamie and Timber turned and suddenly realised they were trapped under its body. Luke saw them slowly disappear from view and called to Bushfire for help. Six dwarfs drove their pickaxes into the spider's side all at the same time, forcing it to lurch back and upwards, enough to allow Jamie and Timber to scramble out, before it came crashing down. It oozed thick, sticky green blood, then deflated like a giant, burst balloon.

'That was close,' said Jamie.

'You are crazy brave!' said Luke.

'Thanks,' said Jamie. 'But I think it's the sword. And Timber, of course.' He rubbed his dog's ears. The other animals stood panting beside him, waiting for the next order to charge. Bushfire ran over to the children. 'We can't do this for much longer,' he said. 'We can keep those spiders busy, but you have to get the other stuff right now, and then we have to leave.'

'That spider's in the way,' said Jamie, pointing.

'Another really big one,' said Jemima.

'There's always another one,' said Luke. 'It's now or never.'

'Right,' said Bushfire. 'Off you go. DWARFS, LET'S GET THE NEXT ONE!' He charged out, roaring orders.

As the injured hobbled and shuffled along the perimeter wall towards the portal, they had to stop now and again to avoid being pierced by talons or crushed against the wall by a spider trying to squeeze through. But many of the spiders looked confused. Some were determined to reach the courtyard and attack, others pushed forward but then just stood there, clacking their claws in the air. Perhaps Vargon's spell hadn't worked on all of them. He certainly looked red-faced and furious on the balcony.

Grizzle was out of view but could be heard bashing a couple of spiders at the far side of the courtyard. At least they were keeping each other busy, though that was not part of Vargon's plan. The next huge spider was very slow and blocking the others from moving forward as quickly as they wanted to. Fights broke out as the spiders at the back continued pushing forward, annoying those further ahead. A few tried to scramble over each other as they surged towards the courtyard, perhaps not even knowing why they were heading there at all. Others turned to fight those behind them.

The dwarfs split into groups and charged at the big front spider from four sides. They tumbled in the air, bouncing off each other to leap high enough to land on the spider's back, careful once again to avoid the poisonous tips. The spider hissed and snapped its teeth, reaching up with its claws to pull the dwarfs off. When that failed, it reared up on its back legs and tried to shake them off.

Jamie and the animals ran low and went for the spider's legs. Luke fired arrows at the spider's eyes, mouth and face to add to the distraction. Jemima and Abigail came out from behind a broken statue and stood right in front of the spider to cast a barrage of Freezing spells, all at the same time. Luke stood beside them and fired arrows at closer range, hoping they would do more damage. Some did, others just bounced right off. Vargon's spell had thickened the spiders' armour, as well as making a few of them smarter.

With an attack on all sides, however, the biggest one was slowly being worn down. He spun around in a last effort to shift the attackers. Two dwarfs were sent hurtling off its back, but the sudden movement annoyed the other spiders even more. The biggest one was furious. It snapped, jabbed and clacked its front talons angrily. Then it lunged forward and snatched at the nearest thing in front of it – Luke, as he reached down to reload his bow.

'Agghhhhh!' he cried, as he was hoisted into the air.

'NO!' screamed Jemima.

Somersaulting from the spider's head, Bushfire and Jugjaw landed just in front of the girls. Bushfire called for two attack pyramids – four on the bottom, three on their shoulders and two on top – with hammers and pickaxes held high. The first group roared a battle cry and charged. The girls looked up at Luke caught in the spider's grip, then they ran closer without really thinking of the danger, firing spells as quickly as they could. The dogs, cats and fox jumped to try to pull Luke out of the spider's claws. They tried to run, jump or claw up the spider's legs, anything to reach Luke and free him. Oberon screeched as he flew close to the spider's eyes, hoping to distract it. Jamie hacked with his sword, destroying one leg in a frenzy, then moved on to the next, all the while thinking that his friend could end up in the spider's mouth.

'ATTACK!' cried Bushfire. The dwarfs on the bottom tier ran in a straight line, holding on to the ankles of the dwarfs above them, and they in turn held on to the ankles of the third tier. The top dwarfs leapt first, onto the spider's head. The next tier threw themselves onto its back, while those on the bottom attached themselves to the spider's belly. The second group did likewise, till the spider was almost covered in dwarfs. They hacked and chopped till it fell.

The spider screeched and dropped Luke, who bounced off the spider's buckled leg and onto the ground. Jamie hauled him up and the two of them hurried over to the wall. They joined the girls who had been forced back by another, smaller spider that had broken through and run around the big one as it collapsed.

Timber collected Luke's bow which had been knocked out of his hand when the spider shook him in the air. Trigger followed, carrying the quiver that had been torn from Luke's back. They sat down with the others, panting, wild-eyed. Then Timber barked at Jamie and stood up as if ready for more.

'We should leave now,' said Bushfire, hurrying over. Timber barked his 'no' bark, then pointed his nose towards the manor.

'I don't think Timber wants to go yet,' said Jamie. 'It's our only chance to get the key.'

'We can't keep the portal open much longer,' said Bushfire. 'We've too many injured, and those spiders keep coming. Vargon might do something *really* nasty, at any moment.'

'There's one thing that might help,' said Abigail. She reached into her pocket and took out the next gem – the opal.

'More gems? Great!' said Bushfire. 'Don't take too long!' he cried, and he ran back to his troops.

The children knew Bushfire was right. They couldn't stay much longer. Abigail held the opal tight, wished for their spells to work, the spiders to go away or something to defeat them – but it didn't work this time. She had wished for too much.

'No!' cried Luke. 'You did what I did at the Crabbage Caves!'

'I'm so sorry,' said Abigail, as she looked at her empty hand. 'There are so many dangers, I couldn't think clearly.'

'Try again, Abi,' said Jamie.

'Wish for a protection shield,' said Jemima.

'Yes!' said Luke and Jamie together.

Abigail held the aquamarine this time. She closed her eyes and tried not to be distracted by Grizzle's roaring, spells backfiring, the dogs barking, spiders clacking and the dwarfs cheering as they took another one down.

'Come on,' cried Jamie. 'Why does it take so long when you need it the most?'

'I know I did it right this time,' said Abigail. 'I'm sure I did.'

'It's getting worse here,' said Jemima. 'Look.'

A number of spiders had started to copy the dwarfs and work in teams. Three of them struck at the same time, spearing three dwarfs as they leapt from another pyramid formation. Other spiders were looking sharper too. On top of that, the two dwarfs who were holding the portal open had been knocked out by lumps of stone Grizzle had thrown, and their replacements were struggling to keep yet another spider at bay.

'I agree with Bushfire,' said Luke. 'We have to leave.'

'No, wait,' said Abigail. 'This gem has to work. The others did.'

At last, a bubble of yellow light surrounded the children, its centre on Abigail, as she had called it.

'Yes!' cried Jamie. 'But Luke's right, we should use this shield to get to the portal.'

They each held a dog, cat or fox and Oberon flew down and landed on Luke's shoulder. Staying very close, they moved towards the portal. But Timber was resisting. He began to growl, then bark.

'We still have to get the gold key,' he barked to the others. 'I'm going into the manor.'

'I'm going with you,' said Teddy, wriggling free of Jemima's grip. 'I have a good idea where it might be.'

Timber broke free from Jamie, and he and Teddy dashed across the courtyard, dodging danger all the way. Oberon flew over the manor to meet them at the back door.

'NO! Timber, no!' cried Jamie after them.

'What are they doing?' shrieked Jemima. 'Teddy, come back!'

'They're after the key,' said Abigail.

The children stopped moving and stared after their pets. Then they looked at the mayhem all around them. More of the bats had returned. They flew in circles overhead, wondering what to do. They didn't like being near the spiders. A few of them had been plucked out of the air, chewed up, then spat out again. Several others were speared and dissolved into dust. Then more spiders joined in the game of catch the bat, giving the children and the rest of the animals an opportunity.

'You're right, Abi. They must be after the key,' said Jamie. 'And we have to help them.'

'The shield is OK,' said Jemima, 'but how long will it last in this place?'

There were shouts of horror from the dwarfs. Two more had been speared after the spiders became bored with bat-killing. Grizzle roared loudly. He had bludgeoned two spiders against the wall, but now he was surrounded, and unfortunately for him, Audmund was nowhere to be seen. Vargon and Zora had also departed.

'Where have the other two gone?' asked Luke, pointing to the balcony.

'I don't care,' said Jamie. 'I'm not leaving Timber.'

'We're all coming with you,' said Abigail.

They headed as quickly as they could, under the shield of light, across the courtyard and back inside the manor. They took the long way around to the back of the building, to make sure they would avoid Grizzle and his next big fight.

Vargon had tried to enchant the spiders a second time, but it had only worked on a few of them. They really weren't ready for battle, as Zora had so clearly pointed out, and there were several flaws in the spells he had used to instruct them. But Vargon knew what he had to do. The next time, his army would be ready, deadly and terrifying, and he would take the battle to the Wandeleis' domain.

Peeking out of his study, Audmund saw the children and the animals run down the corridor and around the corner. He closed his door quietly. 'I do not have time for this nonsense,' he thought. 'If they manage to take the keys it will annoy Vargon, but not me. My goblin friends have already made me perfect copies, one in goblin gold and one in Worfagon silver – and they are certainly not here. My plan is moving along nicely, but I'm not so sure about anyone else's.'

The children and animals stopped outside Vargon's study.

'It's in there,' said Teddy.

Timber jumped on the door and tried to bite the handle. He growled and looked at the children. Jamie looked around for something that might help.

'Would the Reversing spell work?' asked Jemima.

'It's worth a try,' said Luke.

The girls tried it together. It didn't work.

'It is Vargon's study, I suppose,' said Jemima, disappointed.

'We'll have to use another stone,' said Jamie.

'We're using them up fast,' said Luke. 'Try your sword first.'

Jamie whacked at the door handle and tried to drive the tip of his sword into the lock, but nothing budged. 'A gem is the only way we can get the key and leave,' he said.

Abigail took out the sapphire.

'If this doesn't work, we leave,' said Jamie.

'OK,' said Luke.

The girls nodded.

'OK, Timber?' Jamie looked at his dog. 'Last chance, understood?' Timber growled while Teddy scratched at the door. The gem had to work because they had to get the key for the queen. But just before Abigail began her wish, Oberon landed on the ground with the gold key in his beak.

'Look at that!' cried Luke.

Then the eagle flew around the corner. 'Follow me,' he screeched to the animals. 'I'll lead you through the manor so you can avoid the chaos in the courtyard.'

'This isn't a trick, is it?' asked Dougal quietly.

'It was Gildevard who gave me the key,' said the owl.

'I think we have to trust him this time,' said Timber. 'Come on.'

They followed the eagle down the corridor in the opposite direction from the one they had come. The children stayed close together, insisting on holding the animals so that everyone was protected by the shield. Gildevard led them down several corridors, up and down staircases, across halls and around corners until they came to a wide hallway. It was very grand, with tall pillars, four on either side of a black-tiled floor, and two tall blue vases standing either side of the main entrance.

'You'd better hurry,' said the eagle from on top of one of the vases.

'Aren't you coming with us?' asked Timber, looking up at him.

'No,' said the eagle. 'I'll be in touch.' With that, he flew off up the stairs.

Outside, Bushfire was giving new orders. 'Get to the portal and wait for my command.'

'Where are the children?' asked Jugjaw.

'WHAT?' cried Bushfire. 'I thought they were behind that rubble.'

'Nope,' said Jugjaw. 'Oh, look!'

The children and pets moved with the shield out the hall door, down the steps and across the front of the courtyard. Over to the side, they saw Audmund and Vargon trying to untangle Grizzle and one very aggressive spider. The tussle seemed to be amusing the rest of the swarm who had gathered in quite a crush to watch.

The rescue party was at the portal when Ripley scampered out of the bushes. 'Teddy, wait for me!' he cried.

'What?' said Timber. He looked at Teddy.

'Teddy, I helped you. You promised,' said Ripley, looking from one animal to the other. 'Take me with you, please.'

'Why should we trust you?' asked Timber after Teddy quickly explained. 'You've been a traitor before and you've spied on two Wandelei queens.'

'I know, I'm sorry, but Vargon's going to kill me,' he whimpered. 'I have to get out of here.' The squirrel began to sob.

'No more time for talkin',' said Bushfire. He picked Ripley up by the tail and flung him over his shoulder. 'The queen can question him. Everybody out of here, RIGHT NOW!' he cried. The children held on to the animals and Oberon, and jumped into the portal with Bushfire. The rest followed in a crush behind them. The shield faded once they entered the portal, the blue ring of light popped, and the rescue was over.

Chapter Seventeen

THE NEXT STEP

The last two dwarfs were barely through when the portal exploded, collapsing most of the tunnel. Queen Wanda had sent Mrs Emerson to wait by the portal. She hurried the dwarfs into the copse to keep them out of sight. As the tunnel was now completely blocked and it was daylight, the dwarfs would be taking a route through the copse, then on to the far end of a field where they would take a different tunnel back to Hollow Hill.

'We're heading off now,' said Bushfire, still holding Ripley tightly by the tail.

'Thanks for everything,' said Luke.

'You guys were amazing,' said Jamie.

'And we're very sorry you lost some of your friends,' said Jemima.

'It's the job we do for Her Majesty, and the worthy,'

said Jugjaw, looking proud as punch. Timber thanked them with an especially loud howl.

'He's a great dog, that one,' said Bushfire. 'Look after him.' The dwarfs marched off, whistling a victory tune.

'We'll be taking the tunnel from the Allnutts' cellar,' said Mrs Emerson.

'From my house?' said Abigail.

'Yes, your mother gave me a key so I could escort you back to Hollow Hill,' said Mrs Emerson. 'She is working with your Aunt Tamara at Grindlewood House, and Professor Allnutt is busy with Her Majesty.'

'Hey, I don't think we lost many hours this time,' said Luke, looking at his watch.

'Not exactly hours,' said Mrs Emerson. 'You've been gone for three days.'

They walked on in silence.

Tired and a bit confused, they entered the Allnutts' house to go down to the cellar, into the tunnel and on to Hollow Hill. Timber led the way, woofing one minute, howling the next. The animals were in a lively mood. They were very pleased to have Teddy and Jemima back, and to have the keys and the pages for the queen. None of them had been badly injured either, just a few scorches and scratches here and there. All in all, they had been very lucky.

'Gildevard delivered the gold key,' said Teddy. 'That was a surprise.'

'And then he stayed behind,' said Timber. 'I don't understand him at all.'

'Well, it's really good to be back,' said Teddy.

Timber gave his best friend a huge lick. The others did likewise, until Teddy had to shove them off.

'There is something still bothering me, though,' said Timber, after a few minutes. 'Why didn't Audmund stop us? He must have known what we were after.'

'Maybe he knew we'd never get into Vargon's study,' said Teddy.

'Possibly,' said Timber, still wondering about it.

'Do you think he saw Gildevard give us the key?' asked Trigger.

'I don't think so,' said Timber. 'But for such a clever eagle, he takes a lot of risks. I hope he won't stay there too long.'

When they arrived at Hollow Hill, Mrs Emerson said a quick goodbye and Lotus brought refreshments.

'Her Majesty will be so pleased,' she said. 'I'll bring you to see her in a little while.'

'In a little while?' repeated Jamie once Lotus was gone. 'This was an incredible rescue, *and* we got the keys and the pages. Where is everybody?'

'Something else must be going on,' said Abigail.

Luke handed Jamie a plate piled high with sandwiches. 'Eat something or you'll get grumpy.'

'Huh? Oh, thanks.'

They were all hungry, and quickly gobbled down loads of sandwiches, doughnuts and fairy cakes, then washed them down with tankards of fairy lemonade. The animals were glad of their water and food too.

'Look,' said Jemima. 'This is where I hid them.' She unwrapped the bandage around her leg to reveal not only a fully healed ankle – they had already guessed that – but the silver key and the pages.

'That's so clever!' cried Abigail.

'Cool,' said Jamie. 'Um, what about that wand?'

'I haven't a clue,' said Jemima. 'It was in the box of stuff Dad found in the cellar. I had it in my hand when Zora grabbed us. I didn't want the Worfagons to find it so I hid it down the inside of one of the crutches. Later I took it out, thinking it would be great if only I could use it – and it worked!'

'Just like that?' said Luke.

'There's no explanation for magic,' said Jamie. 'Is there?' He looked at the girls, then Luke.

'I've always believed in magic,' said Jemima, shrugging her shoulders.

'It's normal for me,' said Abigail.

'Something has to explain it,' said Luke.

Thaddeus came bustling down the tunnel. He gave Abigail a big hug and a kiss on the cheek, and then he hugged each of the others. Timber jumped on him and received a good rub. 'Wonderful!' Thaddeus said. 'I am so proud of you. The dwarfs came down the field tunnel. They've just finished telling Her Majesty all about your adventure. Come along, she wants to see you.'

They all hurried to the queen's outer chamber, but she didn't look nearly as pleased as they expected. In fact, she looked rather worried.

'Timber, children, well done,' she said. 'Please, sit down.'

Thaddeus sat on a chair, the children on big cushions,

and the animals sat at their feet.

'We found the silver and the gold keys, and the pages,' said Jemima, all excited. She handed them to Thaddeus and he looked them over.

'My, my, you did remarkably well,' he said. 'These are definitely from *The Book of Potions and Spells*.'

'It's good to have them back, but it's a pity the other pages weren't with them,' said Wanda. 'We need them all.' She turned to her fairy-in-waiting. 'Lotus, take the pages to Pearl and her team. They are to begin restoration work immediately.' Lotus took the pages, bowed and left.

'Bushfire and Jugjaw told us what happened in the manor,' said Thaddeus. 'Thank goodness neither Zora nor Vargon got involved. That was my biggest worry, though I expected they might find it beneath them, if you don't mind me saying.'

'They just watched from the balcony,' said Jamie.

'Audmund was there too but he didn't stay long,' said Luke.

'Did you hear or see anything while you were in the dungeon, Jemima, anything important?' asked the queen.

'I heard Vargon getting cross with Zora a few

times,' said Jemima. 'He kept telling her that she wasn't ready yet.'

'And he was furious with Audmund for messing up his plans,' said Ripley. The squirrel was sitting in a small cage in the corner of the chamber.

'Ripley says he wants to make up for his mistakes,' said Wanda. 'I have been considering his request for sanctuary.' She turned to him. 'What do you mean? How did Audmund mess up Vargon's plans?'

'He said he hadn't wanted the keys stolen yet, because Zora wasn't ready.'

'Ready for what, I wonder,' said Wanda. 'An attack, or ...?' She looked at Thaddeus.

'And what is Audmund's plan?' he asked the squirrel.

'No idea,' said Ripley. 'He spent a lot of time in his study. I don't think he liked the others much. In fact, I don't think any of them liked each other at all.'

'He has to be there for something other than making potions,' said Wanda. 'And if he was only meant to steal the keys, he could have handed them over quickly and left. There's definitely more to all this.'

'If Zora is arguing with Vargon, it could mean that

she doesn't like his plan, or that she has different priorities,' said Thaddeus.

'Everything she touches turns red,' said Ripley. 'She's definitely getting stronger. You can feel her power even as she walks past. It's terrifying.'

'She reminded me a lot of Worfeus,' said Jemima.

Lotus returned to the room.

'Please take the squirrel to the lockup, Lotus,' said Wanda. 'We must prepare for an attack on Hollow Hill. Grindlewood garden is also at risk.'

'What?' cried the children. All the animals stood up, on alert.

'Why do you think they'll come to our garden?' asked Jamie.

'History, Jamie,' said Wanda. 'Grindlewood has a turbulent past.' The queen didn't explain further but stood up and walked around the chamber. She stopped and looked at the children's anxious faces. 'I know you've already been through a lot, but we need the pages from *The Book of Darkness*,' she said, more gently. 'Without them, we cannot fully prepare.'

'The Renewal charm,' said Abigail.

'I thought you could only do it at Halloween,' said Luke.

'Halloween is the best time,' said Thaddeus. 'But we could also attempt it at midsummer or the autumn equinox.'

'What about the spring equinox?' said Abigail.

'Yes, that time too,' said Thaddeus. 'But we'd never be ready. It's only a week away.'

'My birthday,' muttered Jamie. 'The twenty-first of March.'

'And it's a long time from March to midsummer,' said Wanda.

'My birthday is midsummer,' muttered Luke. 'The twenty-first of June.'

'And mine is Halloween,' said Abigail. 'And, um, Jemima's is in between the autumn equinox and Halloween. That's weird. All of our birthdays are close to important magical dates.'

'Is it?' whispered Thaddeus. His eyes twinkled over his spectacles, which were perched on the end of his nose again.

The queen smiled. 'You are the *worthy*.'

Professor Flint ran in, quite out of breath. 'I'm sorry, Your Majesty,' he said, 'I thought you should know – Phineas is missing.'

The children and pets went home as the Wandeleis

searched for the spellbound augurer. Thoughts of Mord Manor were still buzzing in their heads as they watched Ernie kiss all the animals' injuries, though not all of them healed immediately. Vargon's dark magic and sinister poisons meant healing would take longer this time.

Thaddeus arrived back late but he was glad the children were still up. They had something important to talk about – Jemima's magic. 'That dimension may have ignited a certain spark,' he said, 'but it would not have been enough for a wand to obey you. And besides, you are not a witch, Jemima, nor an apprentice – until now, that is.'

Jemima shrieked with excitement. 'You mean, do you, I mean …'

'If you can use that wand, then yes, I think we must instruct you. But first we have to find out who it belonged to.'

Jemima reluctantly handed over the wand, after Thaddeus promised to return it as soon as he could. 'Do you still have the Worfagon wand?' he asked.

'No,' said Jemima. 'It went on fire.'

'Ah,' said Thaddeus. 'That was most unusual too.'

Esther brought in a tray of her special night brew –

hot chocolate with melting marshmellows and some other secret ingredient. It was spectacularly delicious. The children enjoyed it then headed up to bed.

Cindy and Sylvie were already cuddled up on the fluffy rug in the girls' room, fast asleep. The Brigadier and Dougal were snoring outside in the kennel, beside a peaceful Trigger. Timber and Teddy went on patrol with Oberon, the wood pigeons and the sparrows.

'Oh, dear, I almost forgot,' said Esther, as she and Thaddeus left the kitchen. 'Arthur phoned earlier. He and Alice are coming home tomorrow.'

'Oh,' said Thaddeus. 'I'd better visit them at the farm before they come over here.'

Vargon had not calmed down. He yelled at Zora, then he roared at Audmund, then he yelled at Zora again. 'This mess was all your fault, both of you! And tell me, who else would have given the gold key to those children?'

'You don't know that Gildevard had anything to do with it,' said Zora. 'Bodric is jealous of him. He might be making the whole thing up.'

'Maybe he's telling the truth for a change,' said

Vargon. 'Where is that pompous eagle, anyway?'

'Hunting,' said Zora. 'I'll speak to him later.'

'And another thing, Audmund,' said Vargon, fuming. 'What happened to those Protection spells? They didn't work, not inside, not outside!' He didn't mention the fact that the spell he used hadn't worked either. 'Let me guess, is the silver key missing as well as the pages from *The Book of Potions and Spells*?'

'It is, My Lord,' muttered Audmund.

'Mistakes, mistakes, I cannot abide mistakes!'

'What about your ridiculous bats and those blundering spiders? said Zora. 'I'd call them mistakes. Even the dwarfs made them look foolish.'

At this point, Vargon was foaming slightly at the mouth, and his bloodshot eyes were almost popping out of his head. 'I told you I will fix those problems,' he roared. 'The spiders weren't ready, just as you are not, just as everything is not! My spiders would have been formidable in battle, a battle in a time and a place of MY CHOOSING! They will be deadly the next time, I promise you. Deadly, and terrifying!'

'I'm tired of waiting for your plan to be ready,' said Zora. '*I'm* ready.'

'I say you are not,' said Vargon. 'And where's that

squirrel? What was he doing here in the first place? This manor is supposed to be under my control. MY CONTROL! MINE!'

'He was spying for us, My Lord,' said Audmund calmly. Then he wished he hadn't said anything.

'*You* were supposed to be the spy, not that rodent. You, Audmund, you and Phineas, you said.'

'Phineas is on his way here,' said Audmund. 'He's following my Calling charm.'

'QUIET! If I see that squirrel again, he will become a new fur collar for my coat. And if that buzzard is lying to you about the eagle, Zora, I suggest you turn him into a feather hat, and perhaps that eagle as well. We can't trust anyone!' Vargon took a deep breath and exhaled slowly. 'Now I'm going to bed.' He limped out of the room.

'Perhaps a wolf would be better than an eagle,' muttered Zora. 'Or even that malamute. Pity he escaped. I'm sure I could have persuaded him to like me.' She sneered at Audmund as she swept past, running her fingers along the table, then down the side of the panelled door. Both turned blood red.

The buzzard had been listening outside the door. Spotting an open window in the hall, he squeezed out just before Vargon stomped out of the room and up the stairs. Bodric settled into a tree and waited for Gildevard to return from hunting. He wanted to catch him before Zora did.

Chapter Eighteen

ZORA'S ATTACK

In the middle of the night, Zora descended the staircase and went quietly to the kitchen. Taking the recipe from a tatty old notebook, she cooked up a special brew. She winced as she forced the first half of it down. 'Trust Vargon to keep all my old notes. Bah! He used to forbid me to take this one. Perhaps he was afraid it would make me stronger than him. Well, it should keep me steady as I shunt across dimensions. I'm not waiting any longer for my revenge.' She drank the rest, draining every last drop, and then removed the evidence.

A twisted smile crept across her face as she returned to her room. Her plans excited her. She put on an elaborate gown, fixed her hair and make-up, then checked her look in the mirror. 'I look good,' she thought. She placed a large onyx ring on her left forefinger, then picked up her wand. Pressing the dark stone with her other forefinger, she shunted in a whirlwind of red to her first port of call.

Zora arrived in a tornado in the middle of Grindlewood Forest. Young trees that were trying to bud were flattened by the force of her arrival. She smiled with delight as she steadied herself, smoothed back her hair and went for a look around. First, she passed the collapsed portal. 'Just as well I don't need that piece of junk,' she thought. She walked a little further and sneered at the sight of her brother's old lair and the cauldron of bones. 'Pathetic!' she cried. 'Oh, enough of this.' Zora stopped, took a deep breath and pressed the onyx ring again. She braced herself for an even stronger whirlwind, one that should take her through all the Protection charms in Hollow Hill.

But something was wrong. Zora felt a bump, then another, and another, then she landed in a crumpled heap in the field at the end of the village. 'Bah! So, they managed to improve their little charms and divert me.

Well, perhaps I can do some damage here first,' and she marched into Grindlewood village.

The wizards and witches who were on duty got the shock of their lives when they suddenly saw who had arrived. Zora stood in the middle of the street, a blood-red cloud whirling around her feet. Her eyes burned with menace and amusement as she blasted everything at will. With every spell, she became bolder. She marched up and down the road, stupefied some of the locals and sent others floating into the sky before letting them drop like stones. She practised a whole range of spells on dozens of people, magical and non-magical, playing with them like they were toys. She set fire to cars and vans and destroyed several shop windows, but it was never going to thrill her for long. 'Time to find the queen.'

Zora fired her wand into the ground just in front of where she stood, blasting a hole in the middle of the road until it reached one of the tunnels under the village. She stepped into the hole, floated down and landed with magical ease. The ground rumbled under the village and under the fields, as the vengeful sorceress stormed through the tunnels to Hollow Hill.

Pendrick was passing through the reception

chamber when Zora announced her arrival with another barrage of Blasting spells. The professor was thrown off his feet and back down a side tunnel.

'Good grief!' he cried, and quickly raised the alarm. Every able wizard, witch, dwarf and fairy hurried to defend their home and their queen. The augurers, who were sworn never to partake in any violent actions, hid in the vault and went into a trance.

Wanda was in her private room. She grabbed her wand and hurried to the reception chamber. As she ran along the tunnels, the four magical keys jangled around her neck. She tucked them inside the front of her dress, out of sight.

When she arrived she found several Wandeleis already injured and the whole place in disarray. Their magic was no match for Zora's even though she wasn't back to full strength. She had been showing off, causing enormous damage with Blaster spells and using Killing spells on anyone who dared to challenge her.

Wanda stepped carefully over the rubble and around the wounded. 'Look after them, Lotus,' she said softly to her fairy-in-waiting. Pendrick approached but Wanda ordered him back. 'No, Pendrick, Zora is here for me.' He was about to protest, but had to dive out of the way, as another Blaster spell hit the wall beside him.

Zora's eyes glowed red as she paced from side to side, waiting for her opponent. 'Call this a palace!' she cried.

Wanda did not reply.

The two queens could not have looked more different. Wanda wore a simple green silk dress that fell softly to her ankles. Zora's outfit for the big revenge was flamboyant and gaudy: a blood-red taffeta gown edged with black, a matching cape, and a new pair of extra sharp and pointy laced-up boots.

'Let's see who the real queen is, shall we?' Zora cried, and she cast her first spell. Wanda ducked and fired back. Both queens fought a fierce duel as the professors and dwarfs lined the walls of the chamber. Now and then the professors tried to cast spells too, but most of them failed or went completely off target, and some wands broke with the effort. Even when the odd one worked, Zora was surprisingly quick at defending herself on all sides, easily blocking any incoming spells. Wanda hadn't met such a skilled opponent, not since Worfeus.

As the fairies attended the badly injured, a few Wandelei witches and wizards tried to help the wounded to safety. In the middle of the chamber, Wanda and Zora moved quickly around as they fired, blocked, fired again, swerved and then stood firm to take sharper aim. The lightning bolts that shot from their wands lit up the room in shades of green and red, as the duel went on and on.

Back in the garden, Timber woke suddenly from a short sleep. He could sense there was trouble. 'Something's wrong in Hollow Hill,' he barked. 'We have to go right away.' He kept barking until the children came out of the house, pulling on their coats and boots. The animals had gathered and Timber was scratching at the fairy house door. Jamie opened it and all the animals dashed in.

'What's going on?' said Jamie.

Timber went straight to the trap door.

'We'd better follow,' said Jemima.

Jamie opened the trap door and Timber charged down and ran on. Teddy and the other dogs rushed after him, nearly knocking the children down as they pushed past. Oberon zoomed over everyone's heads, and Cindy and Eldric scampered past the children's feet. The children followed the animals, running all the way through the tunnels to the reception chamber until they skidded to a halt.

'Stay back!' cried Pendrick.

Wanda saw them too and tried to steer Zora away from the entrance, back towards another tunnel.

But the sorceress had spotted them. She sneered. 'So this is your real army – four children and their pets. How dare you call yourself a queen?'

Again Wanda made no reply.

The dogs were barking and the cats were hissing. Jamie was trying to hold Timber but the dog was too strong. He broke free and launched himself at Zora. He hit her hard from behind and knocked her over. Her wand flew from her hand. She screamed with rage and lashed out with her boot, then grabbed at the ring on her finger. Wanda fired a spell at the ring, but Zora rolled away to protect it.

Dougal and Trigger jumped on her, ripping at her long dress and cape. Teddy and Cindy clawed at her hands. Eldric went for her wand but she called it and it flew back to her hand. She kicked the cats and fox away and aimed at the dogs.

'NO!' cried Jamie, rushing out with his sword.

Pendrick ran out and cast a spell with Wanda to block Zora's Killing curse, then Wanda fired again, directly at Zora. She staggered with the impact, but didn't fall. The children hauled the animals back with help from Bushfire and Jugjaw. They huddled together in a crater blown out of the ground by a Blaster spell.

'Best to stay out of this one,' said Bushfire.

'Good boy, Timber,' said Jamie. 'Now stay.'

Timber growled and barked, and struggled in Jamie's arms. He knew he should obey, but he could sense the queen was worried. He was right. Wanda could feel the magic in her wand fading.

Zora paced across the chamber, back and forth, back and forth, never taking her eyes off her opponent. 'Ready to play some more, little queen?' She didn't wait for an answer, but fired another spell. Wanda dived to one side. It missed her, hitting the wall instead. Huge chunks of rock collapsed. Wanda dodged around the boulders that fell, using them as cover to avoid more spells. Zora simply stood there, firing spells and touching her onyx ring to block Wanda's return fire. Pendrick gulped. The ring was like a second wand – it had powerful magic. His own wand was fizzing uselessly by his side. The last spell he cast had finished it.

ZAP! Another spell just missed Wanda's head.

'Bah!' cried Zora. 'Try this one!' TSSST! another one fizzed by.

Zora kept talking to Wanda, teasing and taunting her. Wanda stayed silent. She took cover for a moment, then leapt out and fired a fierce volley of spells. Pendrick wondered how much longer the queen's wand would hold. After another vigorous bout of duelling, both wands were becoming unpredictable, sending spells bouncing wildly around the chamber. Everyone watching the duel had to duck and dive to avoid being hit directly or by falling debris. Their screams and shouts and sudden movements were all adding to the chaos.

Suddenly, the duel quietened down. Wanda's magic was clearly failing. Her wand wasn't smoking – it looked fine, but she didn't. Her legs felt weak and her face was drawn and white.

'I never thought it would be this easy,' said Zora, and she laughed an evil laugh, then prepared to cast a Killing spell. But her wand blew only a puff of smoke. 'What? WHAT?' she screamed. 'What is happening?'

Looking around the room, she tried to spot who or what might have disrupted her magic. She shook her wand; she whacked it against her boots; she even bit it, but it just smoked.

Wanda almost swooned. Pendrick and Flint ran to her and drew her back.

Zora was left standing in the middle of the chamber, alone, furiously flicking her wand, but it didn't respond. She was feeling dizzy now, as well as angry and frustrated.

'What is wrong with this, this stupid wand? Aaaaaaahhhhhhh! Wanda! Come back! I command you. Finish this duel! Aaaaaaaahhhhhhh!' She walloped the wand repeatedly on the ground.

No one replied. They just watched her. Then the dwarfs lined up and moved forward. One or two were blown back off their feet when their wands misfired, others ended up with blackened faces when the spells failed entirely. The fighting seemed to be over – for now. Then there was a sudden rush of wind and something landed in a swirl of grey. Two strong, old hands reached out of the vortex and pulled the hysterical sorceress inside.

'No, no! I'm not finished with her! I'll be back,

I swear it, I'll be back to finish you off, Wandaaaa!' Zora's voice faded as the whirlwind whipped her away. There was one bright red flash and she was gone. Everyone breathed a sigh of relief.

❦

Vargon arrived back in Mord Manor, where he dumped Zora on the floor of the parlour. 'What do you think you were doing?' he roared. 'I told you you weren't ready. Just look at the state of you – look!' He bundled her over to the mirror in the corner. Then he started to cough. He reached for a small goblet of thick brown liquid sitting on the side table. Grimacing at the bitter taste and lumps of worms, he tried to swallow it quickly then slammed the goblet back on the table. 'Shunting without a portal takes a lot of energy, years of energy if you're not at full strength,' he said. 'That little escapade has taken its toll on you. Be careful, Zora. Just look at me!' He sat down heavily in one of the armchairs. 'If I hadn't pulled you out of there, you would have to begin your recovery all over again. We cannot afford that sort of delay.'

The old warlock was too weak to argue any further. He was shocked by her rash behaviour. Zora wanted to glare at him, but feeling so weak herself, she didn't bother. She looked in the mirror and saw it was true. Her face was more lined, and her hair, having turned blood red over recent days, was now streaked with grey and white. Her skin had a slightly green tinge to it.

'Get some rest and keep taking the red potion, but not the Booster. Yes, I know about that.' He frowned at her. 'I've made a special Power potion for you, a little something from my spider collection. It'll be ready in the morning.'

Zora turned her head slowly to look at him. 'Don't you mean *my* spider collection?' said Zora. 'I invented that Arachnid potion when I was twelve.'

'And I improved it,' said Vargon. 'You were clever then, and more obedient too.' Zora did glare this time, but said nothing. 'If you follow my instructions, Zora, you won't have to wait much longer to achieve everything you desire.'

Back in Hollow Hill, Wanda was greatly disturbed. Zora had felt very strong in the duel. She shuddered to think what the sorceress would be like in time. Her brother had been formidable, but Zora had an extra edge – her raging desire for revenge.

The dwarfs were tidying up after the duel, repairing the chamber as well as several tunnels. The fairies were busy in the infirmary, looking after the wounded. The professors gathered in the queen's outer chamber and waited. Thaddeus had followed from Grindlewood House, when Esther had told him that the whole garden had run down the tunnel. When Wanda came out to meet the professors, she still looked exhausted. Lotus arrived and stood by her side.

'Are the children and animals all right?' asked the queen.

'They're fine, Your Majesty,' said Lotus. 'Pearl is giving them hot chocolate in one of the classrooms.'

'And what of the others?'

'Six dead and dozens injured,' said Lotus.

'Already Zora's magic is stronger than anything we've seen from the Worfagons for a long time,' said Wanda. 'We have to put an end to this.'

'Do the children have any idea where the pages might be?' asked Flint. 'The sooner we can renew our magic, the better.'

'No,' said Thaddeus. 'They were hoping they had

found them all, but they only found the pages from *The Book of Potions and Spells*.'

Wanda sat down suddenly.

'Your Majesty,' said Sparks. 'You really mustn't wear the four keys around your neck all the time.'

'What?' cried Pendrick. 'Your Majesty, you know you can't. They will weaken you.'

'I must wear them to protect them,' said Wanda. 'We may still have a traitor in our midst. It's for the best.'

'Not for you, it isn't,' said Pendrick.

Wanda frowned at him.

'I agree with Pendrick,' said Thaddeus. 'There must be another way to safeguard the keys. Perhaps if each of us took one, then —'

'No, it must be me until we have a better plan.'

'Perhaps you could take them off while we're all here together,' said Sparks, 'to give you a chance to rest.'

'Good idea,' said Pendrick.

Wanda lifted the gold chain over her head and looked at the keys in her hand. 'Very well. For short and safe moments only,' she said. 'Otherwise I must wear them.'

'Your Majesty,' said Lotus. 'As the children are the *worthy*, perhaps they could each guard a key. The magic will not affect them, nor drain their energy, not even Abigail, not yet.'

'It's a dangerous idea,' cried Thaddeus.

'You're both right,' said Wanda. 'Unfortunately, there are bound to be more attacks, to find the keys, to find the orb, and for Zora's enjoyment.' She sighed. 'Thank you, everyone. I will think on it further and let you know my decision.'

Chapter Nineteen

GUARDIANS OF THE KEYS

The weather mirrored everyone's mood for the next few days. It was grey and cool and a steady drizzle was falling – miserable weather for late March. Earlier, Thaddeus had accompanied Luke to Meadowfield Farm to see his parents, who had returned from their family reunion. Thaddeus thought it would be better if Luke stayed on in Grindlewood House for a while, as it would be easier for the four children to be together when they were called upon. Flashing his gold tooth, he persuaded Luke's parents without the need for any discussion.

The Grindles were still in Butterville with Mr Peabody, who every day seemed to come up with something else they had to do or wait for. It was clear they wouldn't be home for Jamie's eleventh birthday, which, with everything else that was going on, had largely been forgotten.

'Memory mist,' said Abigail, gazing out the window. 'Granddad said it's best to mix it with heavy drizzle. Zora's attack on the village gave everyone a terrible shock, especially the non-magical people.'

'At least they won't remember it now,' said Jamie.

'What about all the damage?' asked Jemima.

'The professors fixed it,' said Abigail.

'Um, Mrs Allnutt, now that Luke's parents are back, do you know when ours will be coming home?' asked Jamie.

'It's Jamie's birthday soon,' whispered Jemima.

'Don't worry, no one has forgotten,' said Esther. 'I'm sure they'll be home soon and we'll have lots to celebrate.'

'Butterflies!' cried Jemima.

The trio were hovering outside the window with another message. Timber ran over to them and heard it first, then he went down the garden to tell the other animals. The children went out and the butterflies landed on the girls.

'Hollow Hill,' said Jemima.

The fairies were just leaving the queen's outer

chamber when the children and Timber arrived. Pendrick showed them in. Thaddeus was not present.

'The Wandeleis have four very special keys,' explained Wanda. 'You have already seen some of the magic of the crystal key.' The children nodded. 'The gold key has a number of important uses too, as do the other two keys.' Wanda pointed to them on a table beside her. The iron key was the largest, the crystal key was next, then the silver, and then the gold key – it was very small. 'Together, with a fifth key, they open a pyramid tomb.'

'A *tomb*?' said Luke.

'Who's in it?' asked Jamie.

'No one is buried there,' said Wanda. 'It contains an orb, Othelia's Orb.'

'I saw a picture of an orb in *The Book of Enchantments*,' said Abigail. 'It looks just like a ball.'

'This orb is very important to us,' said Wanda. 'It is so long since anyone laid eyes on it, no one alive today is quite sure where it is or what it can do. But it is the reason the wars broke out between the Worfagons and ourselves, all those years ago.'

'Whoa!' said Jamie. 'That explains a lot!'

'Who's Othelia?' asked Luke.

'She was a very talented Wandelei witch who married a Worfagon warlock, named Oscar. They were forbidden to marry, so they ran away, and stayed on the run for the whole of their lives. It was rumoured that Oscar had captured a super power source and his wife had managed to contain it in a specially fashioned orb. They hid their secret from everyone, because everyone had persecuted them. Time passed and people heard about the orb, a few even saw it, but eventually, no one was left who knew where Oscar and Othelia had hidden it.'

'But they left behind a very intricate puzzle that contains a map to its location,' said Pendrick.

'I have been working on it with Professor Allnutt, since I became queen,' said Wanda.

'This is heavy,' whispered Luke, glancing at the others.

'I guess you need to find the orb before Zora does,' said Jamie.

'Correct,' said Pendrick.

'But who really owns it, if both a Worfagon and a Wandelei created it?' asked Jemima.

'That question has been asked and argued over for centuries,' said Wanda. 'I don't know the answer, but I would prefer if we had it.'

'We don't trust the Worfagons to use its power wisely,' said Pendrick. 'Whatever that power is.'

'So far, we have figured out from the puzzle that these four keys fit four locks that lead the way to the orb,' said Wanda. 'The fifth lock is still a mystery and so is the starting point.'

'What do we have to do?' asked Jamie.

'I want you to be the guardians of the keys,' said Wanda. 'They have been stolen too many times and by too many traitors. We have discussed it and I agree with my fairies, we cannot lose any of the keys again.'

The chamber was very quiet as Pendrick handed out the keys and the children suddenly felt the weight of this new responsibility. Even Timber didn't make a sound. Luke was given the iron key, Abigail the crystal, Jemima the silver and Jamie the gold. Each key was on a simple leather string, which the children hung around their necks, tucking them inside their sweaters.

'Together with the professors and my fairies, we are the only ones who know you have the keys. Tell no one, and keep them hidden. Guard them at all costs.'

After the meeting, the children and Timber headed

back through the tunnels in silence.

❦

After another row with Zora, Vargon left her sulking in her bedroom and went downstairs to the parlour. He was still scowling and muttering to himself as he entered the room, banging the door wide with his walking stick. He was surprised to see Audmund relaxing in an armchair.

'Everything all right, My Lord?' Audmund asked smugly.

'No, it is not!' snapped Vargon. 'Even you can see that Zora is out of control. And why weren't you watching her?'

'I was working, My Lord,' said Audmund.

'*What* were you working on, Audmund? Zora is our priority, nothing else.'

Vargon suddenly grabbed the back of a chair. Watching all his years of planning fall into tatters was putting extra strain on the old warlock, and since Zora's return, he felt worse than ever.

'Zora may be right,' said Audmund, spotting the warlock's frailty.

'About what?' snapped Vargon.

'Perhaps she is ready,' said Audmund. 'Ready to practise, that is, after so much time away.'

'If she is to rule the world and not just that numpty little village,' roared Vargon, 'Zora will need to be able to do a lot more than turn things red and act like a petulant child!'

'Of course,' said Audmund calmly. 'But perhaps she will be in a better mood, My Lord, if she lets off some steam now and again. She has waited a long time, after all. I wouldn't worry too much, not yet.'

Vargon could only manage a scowl.

'Never mind,' continued Audmund. 'I have a solution to her bad behaviour, and you will owe me a great favour in return.'

Vargon scowled again, but he had run out of ideas, so anything was worth listening to. He was horrified, however, when Audmund explained his plan to bring someone back from the dead, using *The Book of Darkness*.

'Are you mad?' he roared.

Audmund didn't answer immediately.

Vargon kept staring at him. He could hardly believe what he had heard. 'So that's what you've been cooking up in your study.'

'It's the only way to keep a sorceress like Zora in check,' said Audmund. 'Soon her powers will be even greater than yours and mine combined.'

Vargon looked around the room as he thought about it. All his years of work, his dedication, his personal sacrifice, and the problem of how to control Zora had led to this rash and dangerous course of action. 'You have a point,' he said. 'Perhaps I will consider it. We will talk about it later.'

'Too late,' said Audmund. 'It's already happening.'

Outside, the eagle landed quietly behind where Bodric was hiding.

'That was sneaky,' said the buzzard, slowly turning around.

'Maybe the Mind-meld has melted your ear-drums,' said the eagle.

'Oh, very funny,' said Bodric. 'Cut the smart talk and listen.' He told Gildevard that Vargon knew the eagle had taken the gold key and that Zora was going to question him about it. The eagle remained calm. 'Don't you recognise danger any more, Gildevard? They might kill you. And what's more, Zora now thinks she wants a wolf for a pet – not you or me. A wolf! Perhaps even Timber himself. Your days are just as numbered as mine!'

'I doubt it,' said the eagle. 'I have no plans to outstay my welcome, even if you'd enjoy getting me into trouble. As for the key, I'll just say I gave it to Timber to earn his trust. Zora will understand. We both know that copies were made.'

Bodric just about managed to hide his surprise when he heard that piece of information.

Then Gildevard changed the subject. 'Did you figure out the message on that parchment I showed you?'

'I did,' said Bodric.

The eagle looked at him with his hunting stare, the one that always made the buzzard gulp. 'Well?'

'It mentioned four keys, five locks and an orb,' said Bodric. 'The iron is first, whatever that means. Satisfied?'

'That'll do,' said the eagle. 'Now, give it back.'

Bodric reluctantly dropped the piece of parchment in front of the eagle. Gildevard picked it up in his talons, scrunching it into a tiny ball. 'You've always been good at encryptions, Bodric, but I don't think I'll need to ask you again. Goodbye.' The eagle flew off, leaving a very disgruntled buzzard behind.

Gildevard wasn't surprised or alarmed by anything Bodric had said about Zora. It wasn't the first time the buzzard had tried to outwit him. Still, he didn't return to Zora straight away. He flew instead to a tall tree outside the manor courtyard and landed well out of reach of any giant spiders. To everyone's relief, they had retreated to their forest nest, exhausted and cranky after their first outing.

Gildevard stuck his head into a small hole in the tree trunk and pulled out a tiny piece of parchment with his beak. 'So, four keys and the iron is first,' he thought. 'Of course! Iron, gold, silver and crystal – the four Wandelei keys – though I've never heard about an iron key before. And what of the fifth? For what? And an orb – could it really be the same one?' He looked at the last piece of parchment in his possession. Could it hold all the answers? He hadn't been able to crack it and he had no intention of risking showing it to anyone, least of all Bodric – not this last one. He would just have to find another way to figure it out. Then, it would definitely be time to leave Mord Manor.

Chapter Twenty

CRYPTO RIDDLES

Thaddeus was in the kitchen with Esther, when the children and Timber arrived back. They all looked worried.

'Do you have the keys?' asked Thaddeus.

'Yep,' said Jamie.

'This is a big responsibility for all of you.'

'We know, Granddad,' said Abigail.

'I'm not happy about this at all,' said Esther, wringing her hands.

'Neither am I,' said Thaddeus. 'But the fairies were very persuasive.'

'The queen told us about the puzzle and the map to the orb,' said Abigail.

'Unfortunately, we don't know if the Worfagons have some way of finding it too,' said Thaddeus.

'If they do have their own puzzles, let's hope they aren't as good at cracking them as you or Luke,' said Jamie.

'The *Crypto Riddles* is Luke's favourite book,' said Jemima. 'He's way better than the rest of us at solving puzzles and cracking codes.'

'Is that so?' muttered Thaddeus.

The phone rang in the hall.

'It's your mum and dad,' said Esther, returning to the kitchen. 'I told them you're both well and everything is fine.'

'Remember, no mention of quests, kidnapping, keys or anything else out of the ordinary,' said Thaddeus. 'Just tell them all the normal stuff you're doing.'

'Normal stuff, um, OK,' said Jamie, trying to think of even one normal thing they had done since their parents had been gone.

Thaddeus beamed his special gold-tooth smile just before Jamie and Jemima ran out to the hall. 'I'm just keeping everyone nice and calm,' he said in reply to Esther's frown.

Jamie did manage to mention a few normal things, like fencing, dog walking and hot chocolate. Then it was Jemima's turn. She was still hoping to have a story written by the time their parents came home, but she hadn't done much writing yet.

'You still have time, Jemima,' said her father. 'We won't be home for another three or four days. Mr Peabody keeps uncovering all sorts of stuff that involves enormous amounts of paperwork, investigation and signatures. It seems my great-uncle George was quite a character!'

'Jamie, Great-Uncle George sounds like a gangster!' said Jemima. Jamie leaned closer to the phone to hear better.

'Well, he did get up to a lot of mischief,' said Greg. 'We'll tell you all about it when we get home. How's the weather there? Any improvement yet?'

'It's still like winter,' said Jemima.

'How's school?' asked Gloria, taking the phone from her husband.

'School? Oh, school is fine,' said Jemima.

'Just the usual, Mum,' added Jamie, nudging his sister.

'As your father said, we shouldn't be too much longer,' said Gloria. 'And we haven't forgotten your birthday, Jamie!'

They said their goodbyes and Jamie and Jemima returned to the kitchen. The others were still talking about puzzles.

'Mr Allnutt wants to take a look at the *Crypto Riddles*,' said Luke.

'You mean he wants to check if you're really as good at puzzles as we said,' said Jamie, teasing.

'He really is, Mr Allnutt,' said Jemima. 'You have to see it to believe it!'

The next day, Queen Wanda and Thaddeus showed Pendrick what they had been secretly working on.

'Queen Cordelia started the puzzle but she didn't get very far because she had so few pieces to work with,' said Wanda. 'Later, Queen Lyra asked me to seek out the missing pieces. I travelled far and wide, searching forests, including Grindlewood Forest, the Eastern Woods, even the Crabbage Caves and other horrid places.' The professors followed her to two large tables covered in small, tattered pieces of parchment: the clues. 'We have enough pieces now to try to solve it.'

'There must be thousands of clues,' said Pendrick.

'There are,' said Wanda. 'Each one carries miniature symbols and codes, in several languages, most of them ancient and rarely used any more.'

'All of them belong to a bigger puzzle – the map itself,' said Thaddeus. 'That's where we made some progress,' he said, pointing to the bundles. 'We know everything in each bundle is one complete piece of the bigger puzzle.'

'But as you can see, it is slow and detailed work,' said Wanda.

'I'm happy to help, of course,' said Pendrick, 'but I was never the best cryptographer. What is it you wish me to do?'

'I want you to write down what we decode onto a master scroll,' said Wanda.

Thaddeus pointed to a chest sitting in a corner of the room. 'My second invisibility chest,' he said proudly.

Wanda walked over to it and unlocked it with a wave of her wand. She took out three long scrolls. 'I started to write it down, but I really need to concentrate on cracking the codes. The fairies are busy with the restoration work, Flint and Sparks are working on more DimLocks, you were taking care of everything else, so Thaddeus and I started working on the puzzle. Now, I need your help with the writing, Pendrick. It must be carefully handwritten, and kept absolutely secret.'

'Of course,' said Pendrick. 'I'll begin right away.'

'We've figured out the order in which the four keys must be used,' said Thaddeus. 'But we don't know where the fifth key is.'

'We don't have a fifth key,' said Pendrick.

'Exactly,' said Wanda. 'It may be another puzzle, but we won't know for sure until we finish it.'

Pendrick unrolled one of the scrolls and read it. 'Extraordinary,' he said. 'It's a pity we don't have anyone else available so we could speed things up.'

'Actually, I think we do,' said Thaddeus.

Wanda and Pendrick looked at him, waiting for an explanation.

'I gave the *Crypto Riddles* to the children over a year ago,' he explained. 'Luke has solved every puzzle in the book. I saw him do it again yesterday.'

'Outstanding!' said Pendrick. 'Could he cope with this one? I mean, I'm sure it's frightfully difficult, and em, can we allow him?' He looked from Thaddeus to Wanda.

'He is one of the *worthy*,' said Thaddeus. 'But we have asked so much of the children already.'

Wanda considered the idea. 'I agree, but let's show it to him and see if he really has the skills. It might be too much for him, or he might spot something we missed. In any case I have another task for the children – we must complete *The Book of Darkness*.'

When everyone had left for the night, Wanda went to the royal safe. It was built into a wall in her inner chamber. She unlocked it and took out a wand made of willow. It was longer than her own Regal wand and had a slim streak of gold down one side. She turned it over in her hands and brushed it against her cheek. It felt smooth and light, disguising the power within. Queen Lyra had found the willow wand too difficult to handle, preferring to use the traditional Regal wand made of larch. Wanda wondered if she would be able to master the willow some day. It had been carved by a Worfagon wand maker in the time of Queen Cassandra, before the wars. Its mood reflected the troubles between the clans, so it would take some time and a lot of skill to master it.

Wanda returned the wand to the safe and took out all the notes her predecessor had left her. Then she thought about the Grindlewood Army. Perhaps it was time to tell them more about the Wandeleis' troubled past. Would they still want to help? And what of Timber? 'He is our protector, Guardian of Grindlewood, so the Ancients have written,' she thought out loud. 'How will he choose between saving our magic and saving the children, if it should come to that?' She went to her outer chamber and asked Lotus to bring the squirrel to her.

'This is your last chance, Ripley. Tell me where the missing pages are.'

'I never saw them, Your Majesty,' insisted the squirrel. 'I never even heard them mentioned. But Audmund is fussy and sneaky. He would have hidden them very carefully.'

'He wasn't very careful with the silver key,' said Wanda.

'He didn't need to be,' said Ripley.

'Explain.'

'He had copies made of the keys.'

'Are you sure? That's no easy task with all the magic they hold.'

'I saw him with a goblin at the edge of Grindlewood Forest when I was returning from, eh, a spying trip,' said Ripley. 'Everyone knows that goblins are obsessed with precious stones and metals, and no one is better at working with gold and silver. I don't know what else he'd be talking to a goblin about. They're not the friendliest creatures.'

Wanda hadn't expected this. It was most disturbing news.

'Both keys?'

'If he was quick about it,' said Ripley. 'I saw Vargon take the gold key from him.'

'And the pages?'

'Like I said before, I only knew they had pages from *The Book of Potions and Spells*. Vargon wanted to check that he had all the right potions for Zora. He was afraid he might have missed something that could help her recovery.'

'All right, Ripley. That is all for now,' said Wanda. 'Lotus, please return the squirrel to the lockup.'

Wanda sat in an armchair and thought it over. 'Maybe Vargon doesn't know that Audmund took pages from *The Book of Darkness* as well,' she thought. 'And if so, maybe Audmund is up to something else. But what?

And the goblin?' She shuddered and frowned.

❧

Thaddeus arrived back from Hollow Hill for an early breakfast the next morning. 'I was helping Sparks with the DimLock throughout the night,' he said. 'He's putting the final touches to it now.'

'We're going after the missing pages next, aren't we?' said Abigail.

The others looked at her. She was one step ahead of them again.

'You really are very knowing, my dear,' said Thaddeus with a smile. 'Yes, that is your next task.' He took off his spectacles and gave them a quick polish. It was becoming more and more difficult to hide anything from his granddaughter. He thought she might be ready for some advanced tuition. 'Now, gobble down that breakfast as fast as you can. The queen wants to see all of you again, and Timber, as early as possible.'

Timber led the way down the tunnels. Everyone was eager to hear the new instructions. They went straight to the queen's outer chamber, where she was waiting with the other professors.

'Thaddeus will have told you of your next task – to return the missing pages from *The Book of Darkness*,' said the queen.

The children nodded and Timber barked. 'The DimLock has been altered so that it will locate Audmund. We believe he stole the pages and still has them. Professor Sparks will explain.'

'I have inserted a small crystal in the centre of the DimLock, which will shine brightly when it is time to travel,' said Sparks.

'You mean the DimLock will know when Audmund is somewhere we can pounce on him?' asked Jamie.

'Yes, when he is alone,' said Sparks. 'But you must be ready to tackle him the instant you arrive, grab the pages, close the DimLock and return immediately. It will all happen very quickly.'

'You mean we only have two minutes again,' said Luke.

'No, you will only have a couple of seconds before Audmund reacts and tries to stop you,' said Sparks.

Thaddeus glanced at Pendrick and the queen. It was another risky plan.

'Are you sure this will work?' asked Jemima.

'The pages must be returned by the *worthy*, and we need them to restore the WABOM,' said Pendrick.

'What if Audmund doesn't have them?' asked Luke.

'We believe he does,' said Wanda. 'But he's been keeping quiet about it for some reason.'

'What about the portal?' asked Abigail.

'You won't need one, this time,' said Sparks. He looked very pleased with himself. 'This tiny crystal makes all the difference!'

'How soon are we going?' asked Jamie.

'The augurers have seen Audmund in a room with Vargon,' said Wanda. 'They seem to be extracting spider venoms, so we don't expect him to be alone again for at least a few hours.'

'We'll send word when the time is right, but make sure you are ready,' said Pendrick.

Wanda turned and went into her inner chamber. Thaddeus followed her, then stopped and turned around.

'Come with us, Luke,' said Thaddeus. 'We'd like to show you something.'

Luke looked a little surprised, shrugged his shoulders at the others, then followed Thaddeus and the queen into the inner chamber.

'Can't we all see the puzzle, Granddad?' asked Abigail.

'I'm sorry, dear,' said Thaddeus, 'only those working on it are allowed in here, and Luke himself will only see a tiny piece of it. We won't keep him too long. The rest of you can go home for a few hours. Luke will follow shortly.'

Jamie, Jemima and Abigail followed Timber down the tunnel to the fairy house, more than a little disappointed.

Luke was feeling both nervous and excited at seeing possibly the biggest, most difficult and most incredibly important puzzle in the world, the magical world.

'Anything we decode must remain a secret,' said Wanda, looking directly at Luke. 'You must not say a word about this to anyone.'

'What about the others?' said Luke.

Thaddeus shook his head.

'Not while we're still working on it,' said Wanda. 'Luke, you kept a great secret for me once before. It won't be that difficult.'

Luke nodded. 'The secret scroll,' he said. 'But I

didn't know the others back then, and it doesn't seem right to keep a secret from them now.'

'If you can't keep this secret, we can't allow you to be a part of this,' said Wanda.

'Oh, OK. I understand,' said Luke, hoping the others would understand too.

'Lotus has set up a separate table for you,' said Wanda. She showed him a big square table in the corner opposite to where she was working with Thaddeus. There was far less parchment on it. 'We want you to work on these particular pieces.'

'Is that all?' asked Luke.

'There may be a few pieces still missing,' said Wanda, 'but not many.'

'Just wait till you take a look,' said Thaddeus, showing him to his seat.

Luke hardly said or heard another word. Once he sat down and turned over the first piece, then another and another, he was hooked.

Chapter Twenty-one

THE FINAL PAGES

Timber called another meeting as soon as they got back from Hollow Hill. He wanted to be sure that everyone was clear on what they had to do before the next stage of the quest. Now that the children were the guardians of the keys, he couldn't be too careful about protecting the garden. He organised everyone into groups; no one was to patrol alone. The dogs, cats and several birds shared the watch on the garden at all times. All the adult rabbits were keeping watch in the rabbit field next door, and in Grindlewood Forest. The foxes and hedgehog split their time between the garden and the forest with all the smaller birds.

The ducks had moved to Lindon Lake, where the heron and several swans had arranged a rota to keep watch. Serena and Swinford Swan had returned with four trusted friends to help out in the garden. Even the bees were awake despite the continuing cold, and they began their chilly spring buzz-around. The garden was on full alert.

A few of the animals gathered at the well, as one patrol took over from another.

'What's happening with Ripley and Bodric?' asked Eldric.

'Bodric might be up to mischief, but not Ripley,' said Timber. 'The queen has locked him up but she's still deciding what to do with him.'

'I hope she doesn't send him here,' said Norville.

'He would have to obey the Rules of the Garden,' said the Brigadier. 'And I'm pretty sure he wouldn't be able to do that.'

Suddenly, everyone was distracted by the arrival of the butterflies.

'Another message,' meowed Sylvie. 'What could it be this time?'

Danni, Darlene and Drew fluttered gracefully over the lawn towards the group. The rainbow butterflies were the only show of colour in the garden so far that spring, but their message was the worst yet:

A darkness is coming, in more ways than one,
It began long ago when great evil was done.
You must right all the wrongs and fight for the
day
When evil is conquered, or the worthy shall pay.

After telling Timber, they flew to the children, who were standing at the door of the fairy house. The message was so bad, they decided to get ready to leave.

'What about Luke?' said Jamie.

'He must know. He's in Hollow Hill,' said Jemima.

'No I'm not,' said Luke, coming up the trap door. 'But I do know. Come on, we have to hurry.'

'Almost ready,' said Jamie. 'Sword.' He strapped it to his side. 'Bow.' He tossed it to Luke. 'Arrows, gems, wands. What else?'

'Oh, no!' cried Jemima.

'What?'

'The professors still have my wand.'

'Never mind,' said Jamie. 'They're not finished checking it yet.'

'How many gems have we got now?' asked Luke.

'Only three,' said Jemima. 'I'll look after them.'

'Crikey, three isn't a lot where we're going,' said Luke.

The four of them stopped for just a second and looked at each other. Everyone had pre-quest jitters.

'Um, how was the puzzle?' asked Jamie, as he fastened his sword.

'Amazing,' said Luke, filling two quivers with silver arrows. 'At first I thought it was like some of the others I've done, but it's not really. Oscar and Othelia must have been very clever.'

'No problem for you, then,' said Jemima.

'The animals have to stay and guard the garden,' said Jamie. 'But I think we should take Timber.'

Timber barked his 'yes' bark. He didn't want the children going anywhere without him, especially now.

'And us,' said Bushfire. The two dwarf brothers popped up out of the trap door. 'Professor Allnutt thought you might like some company.'

'Hey, this is nice,' said Jugjaw, looking around. 'Very cosy.'

'I brought the DimLock,' said Luke. 'Professor Sparks said you're to wear it again, Abigail. Audmund is back in his study.' He handed it to her.

They gathered in a tight circle, Timber in the

centre, Jamie holding his collar.

'On the count of three,' said Abigail. 'One – two – three.' She twisted the locket.

The crystal in the DimLock shone brighter and brighter as everything else around them blurred. The world spun slowly, then faster, then very fast until all seven travellers were off the ground, spinning horizontally, holding hands and Timber's collar. Then it slowed and stopped. The fogginess cleared and they stood in Audmund's study, right in front of him. He froze for a second, but a second was all they needed.

Timber lunged at Audmund, knocking him over, and immediately began searching for the pages in his tunic and cloak. Jamie and Luke quickly covered his mouth and pinned his arms down to prevent him from shouting or using his wand. The girls searched his desk. Bushfire ran to the door and Jugjaw went to the window to keep watch. Gildevard landed on the windowsill outside and peered in, but he didn't make a sound.

'Everyone, stay quiet,' said Jamie in a loud whisper. He and Luke were still holding Audmund down, but the augurer surprised them by resisting strongly. Timber put a stop to that by plonking down on

Audmund's stomach, allowing Jemima to search his pockets. Abigail prepared to cast her newest spell.

'Bindus aurus!'

Ropes appeared around Audmund's ankles.

'Excellent!' said Jamie. 'Do it again, on his wrists.'

'And his mouth,' added Luke.

'Bindus aurus! Bindus aurus!'

Ropes wrapped tightly around the augurer's wrists, and then rows of wide stitches appeared over his mouth, clamping it shut. Timber stood down and the boys pulled Audmund up and into a chair. They searched him thoroughly again.

'Nothing,' said Jamie. 'Can you believe it?'

Audmund was furious. He glared at them, his huge silver eyes bulging.

'We know you have the pages, Audmund,' said Jemima, wagging her finger right in his face. 'And we're going to find them!'

'Good for you, Jem!' said Luke.

Jamie stood glaring at Audmund, his sword raised menacingly. Timber gave a low growl and lunged at Audmund's cape a second time. He sniffed furiously on it and under it, biting and pulling at it till it was ragged. Seeing the eagle was no threat, Jugjaw left the window and searched around the rest of the room. Bushfire remained listening at the door.

'Wait a minute,' said Abigail. 'The pages might be invisible.'

'Then he definitely has them on him,' said Jamie. 'And I think Timber can smell them. That's why he's still at the cape. Go on, Timber, find them.' Timber burrowed through the cape again, much to Audmund's discomfort and dread.

'It must be a secret pocket,' said Abigail, suddenly. 'I saw one in *The Book of Enchantments.*'

'That book is brilliant!' said Jamie. 'Um, how do we find a secret pocket?'

Sure enough, after a further rummage, Timber found something. He scratched and pulled at a spot on the inside of the cape, but they still couldn't see anything.

'Try one of your spells, Abi,' said Jamie.

'Do the Reversing spell,' said Jemima. 'If he sealed the pocket a couple of minutes ago, you might be able to reverse it.'

The sudden look of horror on Audmund's face told them what they needed to know.

Abigail took aim. 'Reversum centrum!'

The secret pocket revealed itself and the folded pages slipped out and on to the floor.

'Yes!' cried Jemima, picking them up.

'Great!' said Luke. 'Let's go.'

'Footsteps!' said Bushfire. Everyone hushed. They could hear the sound of boots passing right outside. They each held their breath till the coast was clear.

'Quick, hold hands!' said Jamie, as he grabbed Timber's collar.

Abigail counted to three once again. She twisted and closed the locket and off they spun, leaving Audmund tied up on his chair. They arrived in the reception chamber of Hollow Hill, very excited.

'That wasn't too bad,' said Jamie, getting up off the floor. 'And those spells are very cool.'

'We were lucky,' said Abigail, blushing.

Pendrick arrived in a flurry. 'Oh, thank goodness you're all right! We were so worried.'

'We're fine,' said Jamie. 'We didn't have too much trouble.'

'But you were gone for a whole day!' cried Pendrick.

'No wonder I'm so hungry,' muttered Jugjaw.

'We thought it only took a few minutes,' said Luke.

'We surprised Audmund, found his secret pocket, grabbed the pages and left.'

'It must be the timer again,' said Pendrick. 'I'll speak to Sparks about it. Come along, you must tell the queen. She'll be very pleased, and so relieved.' He ushered them into her chamber.

'Well done!' she said. 'We were almost planning another rescue!'

'We'll be off, Your Majesty,' said Bushfire. 'We've got some axes to sharpen.'

'Till the next time,' said Jugjaw.

The queen nodded.

'Here they are,' said Jemima, handing over the pages.

Pendrick examined them. 'There is a little damage, a few creases and a long tear,' he muttered. 'But well done, everyone. I think Pearl will be able to repair them. I'll take them to her right away.' He hurried off.

For the first time in a while, Queen Wanda looked relieved, and she was smiling again. 'This is wonderful,' she said. 'As we learned to our cost, the WABOM must be perfect for the renewal of our magic to be complete. We won't make that mistake again. Hopefully, it won't take the fairies too long to complete the restoration.'

'Pearl showed me some of her work before,' said Abigail. 'Maybe I could help her.'

Before Wanda could reply, Thaddeus burst into the room. 'You're back, and you did it!' He gave Abigail a bear hug. 'I'll bet Audmund is in quite a tizzy!' He hugged the others one by one.

'The pages were a bit damaged by all the, um, searching,' said Jamie.

'Never mind, Pearl can do amazing things,' said Thaddeus. 'I'm so glad you're safe and well. It was taking so long, well, I was worried. We all were.'

'Luke, you are a marvel,' said Wanda. 'You solved another piece of the puzzle, which meant Thaddeus and I could finish another part that had been bothering us for ages. Excellent work!'

'I knew you'd be a tremendous help,' said Thaddeus, winking at him.

'Cool, Luke,' said Jamie, nudging him with his elbow.

'All that practice with the *Crypto Riddles* must have helped,' said Jemima.

'I guess,' said Luke bashfully. 'So, um, what did you figure out?'

'Nice try!' said Thaddeus.

'Lotus will organise some supper for you, then you should go home and get some sleep,' said Wanda. 'We'll have more to talk about tomorrow.'

Chapter Twenty-two

PORTALS AND KEYS

The children were in the fairy house when they saw a massive flash of lightning right outside. It hit the well, splintering the bucket and denting the well handle. They had a visitor.

'Look!' cried Jamie.

Timber was on him in seconds, before Audmund even realised where he was. He pinned the augurer to the ground as the other residents hurried over to help. The heron and blackbirds flew over from their lookout posts and the sparrows zoomed down from the roof of the house. They pecked and prodded at Audmund's head and hands while Trigger, Dougal and Teddy snapped and clawed at his feet. Timber snatched his wand and crunched it in half. The augurer shrieked with rage as he struggled to get to his feet. He had intended to arrive at the forest portal, but he didn't know it had collapsed, and he had been diverted to the garden.

The children rushed out to see Audmund still floundering on the ground, surrounded by three furious dogs, two hissing cats and angry birds hovering over his head. Timber stood closest to him, growling menacingly. Jamie drew his sword and Abigail raised her wand.

'What'll we do with him?' asked Jemima, holding a broom and ready to use it.

Before anyone could think of an answer, Audmund mumbled something, then pressed the snake seal on his ring and vanished.

'Hey!' cried Jamie, slicing at the empty space.

'He must be part Worfagon,' said Abigail. The others looked at her, wanting to hear more. 'Magicians who have learned advanced magic can use a ring instead of a portal,' she explained. 'All the senior warlocks have one, but the rings use a lot of magic, so they don't use them very often. I learned about it in my Magical Learning class.'

'Good for an emergency, I suppose,' said Luke.

'That ring means he could turn up anywhere,' said

Jemima, looking around, wondering if he'd reappear nearby.

Jamie petted the dogs, but Timber was very cross. He kept barking and snorting as he trotted around the well. He didn't like someone entering their garden that easily, and now Zora and Vargon would hear about it too – the well was a magic portal to the garden.

'Do you think Audmund really meant to come here?' asked Jemima.

'Good question,' said Abigail. 'He looked really surprised to see us. Maybe he came here by accident.'

'If it was a mistake,' said Jamie, 'where did he want to go?'

'Hollow Hill?' suggested Jemima.

'Not after Zora's visit,' said Jamie. 'Though maybe,' he said, after thinking about it.

'How about the forest?' said Luke. 'The broken forest portal might have sent him here instead.'

'Genius!' said Jamie.

'And he could have used the ring to try and go there now,' said Abigail.

'Let's take a look,' said Luke.

'We should take the dogs,' said Jamie. He looked

around. Timber was already giving the other animals instructions.

'If word gets out that our well is a portal, we may get some unwanted visitors,' he barked. 'Teddy, you're in charge. Make sure everyone is on high alert and stay close to the well.'

The dogs ran ahead across the field to the forest while Oberon scouted overhead. The children passed the spot where the first portal had exploded, near Worfeus' old lair. They took a look around.

'No sign of anything,' said Jamie.

'He might have just gone back to the manor,' said Abigail. 'Using that ring could make him feel unwell. He couldn't keep hopping about without using a portal some of the time.'

'He could have gone to another portal, but we don't know where all of them are,' said Jemima.

Luke examined the cracked portal stone. 'Some of these symbols are definitely in the puzzle. Oh! I shouldn't have said that.'

'Never mind, tell us what they mean,' said Jamie.

'He can't tell, can you, Luke?' said Jemima.

'Nope,' said Luke. 'They made me promise. But I

also saw some of them in the *Crypto Riddles* book and as we've all looked at that before …'

The others waited for him to say something incredibly important.

'But it takes a while to work out each puzzle,' said Luke.

'Oh,' said Jamie. 'Sounds complicated.'

Oberon flew down and then through the hanging ivy that covered Worfeus' lair. The dogs hurried after him.

'Hey, come back!' cried Jamie, crawling in too. The three dogs were sniffing and digging at the back, while Oberon was scratching at the lump of granite he had found before. He squawked excitedly. Jamie touched the stone and could feel that there was something written on it, but he couldn't see properly in the dark.

'Luke, take a look here,' cried Jamie. 'More symbols.' The others bundled in behind Jamie.

'Did anyone bring a torch?' asked Luke. No one had.

'I'll try to light my wand,' said Abigail.

They had to reshuffle to allow Abigail to get to the back of the lair. 'Luminatus!' she cried, and shone the wand light on the stone.

Oberon was staring hard. He thought he spotted something, though it was cleverly disguised within all the overlapping symbols. 'Timber, do you see that? I think it's a lock.'

The owl was so excited he started flapping his wings a lot, forcing the others to lean back. Timber kept turning around to look at Jamie, then back to the stone and back to Jamie again. With all his movements and Oberon's flapping, everyone was bumping around in the small space.

'Do you recognise anything?' asked Jemima from the back.

'I saw some of these symbols in the puzzle too,' said Luke. 'Others are different though.'

'What's that in the middle?' asked Abigail.

'Timber and Oberon seem to know,' said Jamie. 'They're very excited about it.'

'Maybe it's got something to do with what Wanda said to Timber,' said Jemima.

'That's a clever idea,' said Jamie. 'It could be.'

Timber's 'yes' bark was extra loud this time.

'Wait a minute,' cried Luke. 'That's a lock! It's so close to the other symbols, you can hardly see it.'

At the mention of a lock, Timber licked Jamie

several times. Oberon landed on Luke's shoulder and rubbed his head against his neck.

'Crikey,' groaned Jamie. 'They really do know something, but what?'

It was becoming so hot and stuffy, the children decided to crawl out for a minute to get some air, but the dogs and Oberon stayed where they were. Dougal and Trigger bounded into the lair, dying to know what was going on and wanting to have a good sniff around.

'We found something,' said Timber.

'It's a lock,' said Oberon. 'Perhaps one of the keys will fit it.'

Dougal and Trigger sniffed around the stone.

'It could be even more than that,' said Timber.

They waited for him to continue, but he seemed unsure all of a sudden.

'Oh,' said Oberon, looking at Timber. 'One of Wanda's secrets?'

Timber looked at him.

'Well,' began Oberon, 'if it makes you feel better, it was Jamie's idea to come here. I found this stone and you followed me in here. Then I figured out there was a lock in the middle of it, so you didn't really tell us any part of the secret, did you?'

'Sounds about right,' said Timber. 'Now that we have found it, it's better that you know exactly what it is. Wanda told us about a puzzle-map that leads to an important treasure called the orb. She's still working on the puzzle with Thaddeus, Pendrick and now Luke too. I think this might be where it starts. And I think I know which key goes first – but that is a secret.'

'Of course! said Oberon. 'Oh!'

'That's why Luke was so quiet,' said Trigger. 'He's always quiet when he's doing a really difficult puzzle.'

'It's better that we all know about it before someone else finds it, someone like Bodric, or even Gildevard,' said Dougal.

They went outside to the children. They were all wondering the same thing. A lock. Four keys. Which key? And they didn't really know much about the orb, nor had they been asked to find it.

Luke pulled the iron key out from under his sweater. 'I think this one's first,' he said. 'In fact, I think I know which one is first, second, third and fourth.'

'But you're not allowed to say,' said Jemima.

'Well, I think I can,' said Luke.

'How come?' said Jamie.

'Because I didn't find out from the puzzle,' said Luke. 'That would be OK, wouldn't it?'

'No idea,' said Jamie. 'Tell us anyway.'

They looked at each other, excited but a little spooked too. Luke beckoned for everyone to huddle close together, even the animals. Oberon flew onto Luke's shoulder as he explained his idea in a very low voice.

'You remember when the queen showed us the four keys,' he said. The others nodded. 'They were laid out in a particular order on the table beside her: iron, crystal, silver, then gold – biggest to smallest. This lock is definitely big enough to take the iron key but too big for the other keys.'

Silence.

'So, what do you think?'

More silence.

'I say that's very clever of you, and let's see if your key fits,' said Jamie.

It didn't take long for the others to agree, but Abigail had a warning.

'You only get one chance to try a key in a magical

lock. If you get it wrong, an enchantment could seal the lock, or a curse could rebound, or something awful might happen. You must be sure.'

The children and Timber went back into the lair. Timber pushed past the others to the back, and sat down beside the stone. Luke turned the iron key in the lock and the stone slid over to one side. It revealed a narrow stone staircase, hewn out of the rock below. Timber hopped through the hole and onto the steps before anyone could stop him. Whatever was down there, he would meet it first, especially if it was something bad. Oberon flew around the children's heads and followed Timber.

'Let me go next,' said Jamie. 'I've got this.' He crawled to the hole in the wall, holding his sword in front of him. He eased himself through the gap and went down a few steps. It was pitch dark. He waited for Abigail so her wand could light the way. The others followed, moving tightly together, slowly and carefully down the narrow staircase. When they reached the bottom, there was nowhere to go except straight on.

'OK?' asked Jamie.

Everyone nodded. Timber continued at the front.

The passage narrowed so much that the children had to walk sideways for a while, before it widened out again. All the while, it continued to slope downwards. They reached a sharp turn, and then a few more tight turns after that. After walking for another minute or so, they arrived at a dead end. Only a block of granite faced them. It was covered in symbols like the ones they had seen on the first stone, and some new ones too. They all tried to look, but it was impossible in the tight space.

'This one has a lock too,' said Jamie. 'I guess it's your key next, Abi.'

'Crikey,' said Luke. 'The fairies must have designed this place.'

'It's like a tiny upside down pyramid,' said Jemima. 'It seems to get steeper and narrower, maybe it'll reach a tiny point.'

'The Pyramid Tomb!' said Abigail. 'Maybe we will find the orb!'

'Wow!' cried Jamie. 'I think you're right. I say we go all the way to the end.'

'You know, Timber and Oberon seemed to know about this lock already,' said Luke.

'And we have the keys,' said Jamie.

'And you know the symbols,' said Jemima.

'Then maybe we were meant to find it,' said Luke.

Abigail pulled out the crystal key. 'I think you should check the symbols before I put the key in, just in case.'

Luke moved forward and checked each symbol, trying to remember all those he'd seen before, in the books and on the queen's parchment.

'Whoa!' he said. 'You're right, Abi. There's a second puzzle here alright. I think there is a sequence to follow before we use the key, or maybe after.'

'It's nearly always before,' said Abigail.

'Nearly?' muttered Jamie.

Luke worked out the sequence quickly. 'There, that should be it,' he said.

Abigail inserted the crystal key into the lock and the stone swung slowly back with a deep groan.

'That sounds so spooky,' whispered Jemima. Everyone had goosebumps. Oberon's sudden toot made them all jump, and the boys bumped their heads on the low ceiling.

'Ouch!'

'Ooooh!'

'Look! The passageway splits in two,' said Abigail,

sticking her wand through the doorway to see what lay ahead. 'Which way should we go?'

Timber trotted ahead and sniffed around. Oberon was well able to find his way in the dark. He flew down one passageway but returned quickly.

'That one's a dead end,' he tooted to Timber. Both Timber and Oberon headed down the other one, the children close behind them.

They followed more twists and turns and avoided more dead ends after Oberon scouted ahead. It was getting decidedly warmer as they walked deeper underground, which was a little unnerving, and the ceiling was now so low they had to crouch.

This time, they came to a very small door, once again covered in symbols.

'It's your turn, Jem,' said Jamie.

She took out the silver key and waited while Luke figured out the next sequence. He took a little longer this time. Jemima was about to turn the key when Luke cried out.

'Wait! I think I missed something.'

Timber barked so fiercely he made everyone jump.

'What's wrong?' asked Jemima.

'I know I got the sequence right,' said Luke. 'But I

think it needs a password as well. I missed it the first time. I'm really sorry.'

'Whoever made this place was very sneaky,' said Jemima.

'Can you figure it out?' asked Jamie.

'Yes, I've got it,' said Luke. 'But I want to double check it, just to be sure.'

'Please be sure,' said Abigail.

A few minutes passed.

'OK. That's it.' Luke pressed five symbols, one after the other. Jemima took a deep breath and turned the key in the lock. The door squeaked open.

'Three down, one to go,' said Jamie.

They passed through the little doorway and stopped. The passage split in five different directions.

'Off you go, Oberon,' said Luke. The snowy owl flew off and back a few times, tooting to Timber each time he returned. The fifth time, Timber barked at Jamie, then bounded off down one of the tunnels. The children were about to dash after him, but he disappeared into the darkness. Jamie called after his dog, but they could no longer hear him or Oberon at all. They stood there in the darkness, wondering what had just happened.

'Let's start down this passage,' said Jamie. 'I think that's where they went.'

'I thought they went down that one,' said Jemima, pointing to the left.

'Seriously?' said Jamie.

'I thought it was that one over there,' said Abigail, looking at a different route.

They argued about which was the right one for quite a few minutes. They were all feeling a bit panicky, and worried about Timber and Oberon.

'Hey, here they are,' said Luke, much to everyone's relief.

Oberon tooted loudly as he flew towards them, then Timber bounded out of the darkness, straight up to Jamie. He licked his hands excitedly.

'You gave us a terrible fright,' said Jamie, hugging his dog. Timber woofed, turned around and trotted down the right hand passage. The children followed as quickly as they could, but the passage became much more difficult to move in. It curved tighter and tighter and became lower and narrower, forcing all four children to crawl. Finally they arrived at a tiny door. There was no mistaking it; something very special was behind it.

Chapter Twenty-three

THE ORB

All the symbols that adorned the door were made of gold, just like the lock.

'This is it,' said Jamie. 'The gold lock for the gold key.' He took it out.

'Wait!' the others cried all together. Jamie turned his head.

'What now?'

'We don't know, do we?' said Abigail. 'If this is the final lock, there must be another puzzle, an enchantment, something.'

'But it's not the final lock, is it?' said Luke. 'There's a fifth, and we don't have a fifth key.'

'Maybe it's not a key,' said Abigail.

The others looked at her. Perhaps she was right. The fifth key could be anything, as it was the final barrier to the orb.

'We can't know what the fifth key might be until we get past the fourth,' said Jamie.

That made sense to everyone. They crouched uncomfortably, while Luke spent quite a while figuring out the puzzle on the door. After what felt like hours, he cracked it. 'Ready!' he said with a big grin. 'That was a tough one.'

'Um, are you sure you got it right?' asked Jamie.

'As sure as I can be,' said Luke.

'Right, let's do it,' said Jamie.

He put the key in the gold lock and waited for Luke to dial the code. As he touched each symbol, the gold shone brightly. Then Jamie turned the key. The door slid to the side, revealing a tiny cave-like space behind it.

Each of the children tried to get in, but none of them could fit, not even Abigail. Timber managed to squeeze through only with a lot of pushing and shoving from Jamie. Finally he got through the little gap and he and Oberon took a look around. There wasn't much to see. It was a very small, round, dark cave with a stone on the ground in the middle of the space. Again, the stone was granite and looked quite like the one back in the lair. Luke took Abigail's wand

and, lying on the ground, held it into the cave as far as he could reach.

'There's something on that stone, but I can't make it out. It doesn't look like any symbol I've seen before.'

'Let me have a look,' said Jamie. 'Crikey!' he cried after a moment, turning too quickly and bumping his head again.

'Ow, yeowch! That's so annoying!'

Timber was still sitting by the stone and he kept barking as Oberon pecked around the single symbol on the stone.

'What is it?' asked Jemima. 'And what's up with Timber?'

'It looks like a paw print!' said Jamie.

'Timber!' cried Abigail.

'What?'

'It could be for Timber's paw.'

Timber stopped barking and looked at Jamie. Jamie looked at the stone again, then at Timber.

'I think Timber agrees with you, Abi,' said Jamie. 'But what's going to happen when he presses his paw on the stone?'

After much discussion, the children couldn't decide if they should let Timber do it or not. Jamie was worried that something bad might happen to him, and none of the children could get inside the tiny cave to take a better look and see if there were any other symbols, codes, puzzles or anything else. It was impossible to know what they should do next.

Timber and Oberon were talking about it too, but they wouldn't leave the cave until they had made a decision. Timber felt sure his paw would fit the imprint on the stone.

'If we find the orb, it will be a real triumph for the queen,' said Timber.

'I agree,' said Oberon. 'But this is risky, Timber. If it's not for your paw, who knows what will happen.'

'Trust me, Oberon.'

Timber turned and licked Jamie's outstretched hand, howled loudly, then placed his big wide paw on the stone.

It sank into the ground a few inches, and then there was a loud, grating noise as another stone, hardly visible in the wall, moved slowly to one side. A light shone out, growing brighter and brighter as the stone pulled back, blinding everyone for an instant. When their eyes adjusted, they saw it clearly – Othelia's Orb. It resembled a glass ball, covered in a gold lattice, like a fine gold lace stretched over its surface. The light coming from inside was very bright, changing colour all the time and darting around inside the orb like it was trying to escape.

Timber howled and Oberon tooted, while the children cheered with excitement and delight. But they were silenced quickly when Timber gave a frightfully loud bark, his danger bark. The orb began to move, or rather, the little plinth on which it sat began to move out of the wall and into the tiny cave. It stopped in front of Timber, as if waiting to be lifted off. Should they take it? How could Timber carry it? Was it safe to touch? Was it really Othelia's Orb, or just some other orb?

'I think we should leave it here,' said Abigail, sensing everyone's doubts.

'Maybe you're right,' said Luke after a moment. 'We're the only ones with the keys, so no one else should be able to get to it.'

'And only fairies, birds and animals could get in this far,' said Jamie. 'Even Timber had to squeeze in. He's covered in muck, and eh, so are we.'

'And Luke's the only one who knows how to decode the symbols on the doors,' said Jemima. 'No one else knows all these things, and anyway, where would we put it that would be safer than here?'

That was the real problem. Finding it was a great achievement, but keeping it safe would be another matter altogether. Either way, Timber decided for them. He pressed his paw on the paw print again, and the plinth slid slowly back into the wall, taking the orb with it. The door closed over and the light was gone.

'That's decided, then,' said Luke.

'I think Timber's right,' said Abigail.

'Me too,' said Jemima.

'Good boy, Timber,' said Jamie, as he pulled his dog out of the doorway of the cave. 'Time to go home.'

It was difficult to turn around in the tight space, but they managed it, turning one by one, dodging Oberon as he fluttered past them, and trying not to trip over Timber too. Each door had locked automatically once they pulled it shut, and so everything was left as they had found it.

It was a quiet walk back to the lair in the forest. Everyone was a bit dumbfounded by what they had discovered. It was another huge secret they had to keep.

They were all very grubby when they finally emerged into the forest. To their surprise, Gildevard was perched in a tree outside the lair, motionless as a statue.

'Find anything interesting?' he asked.

'Just exploring with the children,' said Timber.

'Hmm, that's what Trigger and Dougal said, though I'm surprised they didn't go with you.' He stared at Timber, daring him to say something more, but Timber was not to be tricked. 'Never mind, I just thought you'd like to know that both Zora and Vargon are tucked up in their beds, guzzling potions.'

'Serves them right,' said Oberon, scowling at the eagle. 'Too much dimension hopping and turning up where they're not invited.'

The children came out of the lair one after the other. Luke came out last after he turned the iron key in the lock and the granite stone slid back into place with a thud. They left the eagle sitting there and headed back to the garden.

Bodric had been hiding nearby, his scent protected by the shunt stone that Audmund had given him. He smiled to himself. Zora would like to hear about this. It might even win him her favour again.

Timber decided to tell the other cats, dogs and Eldric about the orb, but not all of the residents. He thought it would be too troubling for some of them, and they were already worried about Zora. The children changed out of their grubby clothes and gathered in the fairy house. They were all still thinking and talking about the orb.

'Did we really do the right thing, leaving it there?' asked Jamie, as he gave Timber a vigorous brushing.

'I think so,' said Jemima. 'If it really is Othelia's Orb, and it wasn't discovered for such a long time, it should be safe where it is.'

'Timber seemed very sure, didn't he?' said Jamie.

'I don't think you could have stopped him pressing the stone, not the first time or the second,' said Luke.

'We probably should tell Granddad,' said Abigail. 'It might be too important not to.'

'And then he can tell the queen,' said Jamie, 'in case she's cross with us for finding it, and leaving it there, or just finding it at all.'

Everyone agreed.

'Come on, let's check the books for orbs,' said Jemima. 'We might spot something, now that we know what we're looking for.'

They pulled down all their favourite books from the shelves, and started turning the pages.

Chapter Twenty-four

THE DESTROYER SPELL

Vargon stopped outside Zora's bedroom, pausing for a moment to muster what little energy he had. He felt dreadfully weak after the last shunt, and it was taking longer than usual to recover. Zora took her time opening the door. She knew what her tutor wanted to talk about.

'We need the orb, Zora,' he said, standing in the doorway. 'It's our only real guarantee of success – and unlimited power. At least wait until we have it in our possession before you do anything rash.'

'I'm not waiting any longer,' said Zora.

'It won't be much longer,' said Vargon.

'Leave me,' said Zora, with a dismissive wave. She shut the door in his face and returned to her preening. This was going to be her big moment, her revenge, the destruction of Hollow Hill and its queen. No one was going to ask her to wait. She looked at the collection of empy goblets on her dresser. She had drunk a considerable amount of potion over the last two days, but the effect would be short-lived. She had to act immediately, before it wore off.

She put an extra dab of red lipstick on her mouth. 'Mmm, gorgeous!' Satisfied with her make-up, she put on her new outfit. It was her most flamboyant gown yet – blood-red satin, with lots of sequins and ruffles. She had a long red cape to match and a pair of shiny red ankle boots. Her hair was various shades of red now, dry and unruly, and streaked with grey. This annoyed her intensely, but she managed to tame it by weaving it into an elaborate bun piled on top of her head. Then she added her final touch of glamour – several gaudy hair pins shaped like spiders and snakes.

Zora stood back and admired herself in her new wall of mirrors. She pulled on her long, black leather gloves, then gulped down a final concoction of spider blood, snake venom, thistles and herbs. 'That'll keep me going till I finish the job,' she thought. 'And I'll use the portal this time to save my energy for the real fun.' She practised a few sneers, picked up her wand and headed outside.

The red queen whirled into the reception chamber of Hollow Hill with flashes of red lightning and violent gusts of wind. She brought hundreds of vampire bats and metal hawks along to keep the wizards and witches busy. Zora alone would deal with Wanda. After all, she had to prove to herself and to everyone else that she was a more accomplished witch than her opponent, and therefore a better queen. The bats and hawks circled her, their flapping echoing through the tunnels as she marched confidently towards the Forest Queen's outer chamber.

Hollow Hill was unusually silent. She sneered at its simplicity and lack of adornment. As she crossed the chamber, back and forth, her flashy red gown swished around her ankles. Her pace quickened as her impatience grew. She knew Wanda would be aware of her arrival, and she didn't like to be kept waiting. The bats circled high above, blocking out the ceiling like a billowing black sheet. The hawks clustered in the corners, their metal wings eerily reflecting the candle light.

'Looking for me?' said Wanda from behind her. Zora twirled around and fired instantly. CRACK! CRACK! CRACK!

Wanda had expected a strong opening move and blocked the triple-spell.

Once again, she looked so dramatically different from her wild-eyed opponent. Dressed in shimmering lilac silk, Wanda moved gracefully and silently towards her enemy.

'I see you've brought your little helpers,' said Zora, pointing to the dwarfs who were gathering at the mouths of the side tunnels. 'And I brought mine.' The bats and hawks immediately swooped to attack the dwarfs.

CRACK! CRACK! from Zora's wand.

Wanda blocked the double-spell and joined her opponent in the centre of the room. Wizards and witches entered the chamber and lined up against the walls. They would not get involved in the duel of the queens, but they would have to deal with the hawks and the bats.

Wanda and Zora fired their wands at exactly the same time, sending sparks flying around the chamber. They both dived to avoid being hit, quickly turning to fire their wands again and again and again. Soon the room was lit up with spell fire, coloured smoke and the smell of scorched earth, wood and cloth.

CRACK! WHIZZ! CRACKLE!

SIZZLE! CRACK! BANG!

Back and forth, they battled fiercely. As the duel hotted up, they screamed their curses and spells ever louder. Furniture in the chamber was set ablaze, and candles exploded. Shot after shot flew across the room, often bouncing off walls and landing somewhere unexpected. Onlookers shrieked and dived for cover as the duel raged. Injuries began to mount from deflected spells, chunks of earth falling off the walls and ceiling, and a few hawks exploded too, sending shards of steel slicing through the air.

CRACK! CRACK! CRACK! from Wanda's wand.

BANG! WHIZZ! SIZZLE! replied Zora's.

So it continued.

Back in Grindlewood garden, Timber suddenly stood and sniffed the air, his ears twitching. He sensed grave danger. 'The queen's in trouble!' he barked. Then he jumped on Jamie and ran to the fairy house. The children followed and many of the animals and birds bundled in too. 'Wait!' barked Timber. 'Some of you must stay here.' The animals and birds obeyed and quickly went back to their posts. Only the dogs, cats and Oberon remained.

The children got organised. Luke took his bow and arrows off the wall. Jamie clipped his wooden sword to his belt. Abigail grabbed her wand and Jemima checked her pocket for the pouch of gems. Jamie opened the trap door but had to move out of the way as the dogs and cats rushed down first.

'Yikes!' he said. 'This looks bad.'

'I'll follow you in a minute,' said Abigail. She ran back into Grindlewood House, where her mother and aunt were mixing healing potions and creams. 'Something's happening in Hollow Hill,' she said, bursting into the kitchen. Esther and Tamara were already on alert as Nura Nightingale was screeching in her cage. 'All the animals went charging down the tunnel. Timber seems to know something is wrong and I feel it too. Where's Granddad?'

'He's with the professors,' said Esther. 'I'll send Nura ahead.'

'It must be Zora,' said Tamara.

Esther whispered to Nura and released her out the window. 'Abigail, wait! I'm coming with you,' Esther called as she stuffed some of the medicines in her coat pockets, grabbed her wand and ran after her daughter, with Tamara close behind.

The animals and Oberon had arrived ahead of the children and they leapt in to defend Hollow Hill. The bats had been improved by a new spider venom. They were smarter this time and their talons had poisonous tips, just like the spiders – much smaller but just as deadly. The dwarfs went after them with their hammers, wands and pickaxes. The witches and wizards joined in too, but many spells were misfiring and backfiring, causing pockets of thick smoke to appear around the room. Many Wandeleis were stabbed by beaks or poisoned by talons. It was all-out mayhem in the chamber, and yet Wanda and Zora concentrated on each other in the centre of the room, as if nothing was happening around them and no one was there at all.

When the children arrived, they burst into the action. The animals were already busy with the hawks, while the dwarfs were concentrating on the bats. Jamie leapt up with his sword, slashing and cutting down bats and hawks alike. Luke and Jemima tucked in behind a few overturned chairs and got themselves ready. Jemima was feeling rather useless.

'If only I had my wand!' she cried. 'I could do something to help.'

'Never mind,' said Luke. 'You can spot trouble, and reload the quiver for me.'

'Aaaghh!' cried Jamie, as he appeared through a cloud of purple smoke. Several bats fell around him. He turned and struck a group of hawks just as they came in low to strike. 'Don't get scratched by the bats. I think those red claws are poisonous!' Through gaps in the smoke, several of the injured could be seen writhing in pain on the ground. 'The animals are keeping the hawks busy, so you and I should aim for the bats.'

Luke nodded to Jamie and fired a few more arrows.

Jamie then called to Abigail. 'Can you stun them, Abi?'

Abigail scurried over. She had already cast her entire range of spells. 'Only some of my spells are working,' she cried. 'The magic is definitely weakening.'

'I really wish I had my wand,' cried Jemima.

'I have it here!' shouted Thaddeus, as he and Pendrick entered the chamber, followed by a rather breathless Flint and flustered Sparks.

'It's OK?'

'Yes, take it!' said Thaddeus. 'I'll explain everything later.' He and Pendrick hunkered down in another corner and blasted a group of hawks. The hawks melted in mid-air and everyone had to scurry out of the way to avoid being burned by dripping steel. Flint and Sparks went to help some of the dwarfs who were getting into trouble with another group of hawks.

Abigail and Jemima huddled together and fired a host of spells – wobbling, freezing, jellying and melting – confusing enough bats and hawks to give Jamie, Luke, Pendrick and Thaddeus the chance to finish them off.

The chamber was full of backfiring spells, clouds of smoke with stink-bomb odours, crackling and fizzing, small fires breaking out, and lots of barking, yelling and shouting. All the while the duel of the queens continued.

In amongst the chaos, Esther and Tamara were hurrying around the wounded. Esther grabbed Jamie by the arm. 'My wand went on fire,' she cried. 'We need your help.' She pulled a bottle out of her pocket. 'It's an antidote for the red venom. Follow us.'

Jamie ran with them, fighting back bats and hawks

who spotted what Esther and Tamara were up to. The two sisters worked their way around the room. But something wasn't quite right. Jamie felt his sword buckle.

'Something's wrong,' he yelled to Esther. 'I'm not sure I can stop them.'

'Dark magic feels different,' cried Esther. 'Keep at it.'

One of Zora's spells misfired and bounced off a wall. Jamie ducked and raised his sword like a shield, deflecting the spell to the ceiling, where it blitzed several bats and hawks.

'Whoa!' he cried. 'That was lucky!' Then he thought his eyes were playing tricks on him, as his sword faded till he thought it was going to disappear. 'Don't turn back to wood, not now!' he cried, then suddenly the steel shone brightly again. Relieved, he ran after Esther and Tamara, who were trying to help two dwarfs who were on fire.

'Stupificus totalis!' cried Jemima.

'Jellitorum limbus!' cried Abigail.

'Superb!' cried Luke. He fired off more arrows and then Jemima used the Retrieving spell to replenish Luke's quiver. 'Another great spell!' cried Luke.

Timber, Teddy, Dougal and Cindy were all battling bats and hawks. There were so many of them, yet the animals fought bravely and tirelessly. Despite the floor being covered with dead dust, the bats and hawks didn't seem to reduce in number. The animals battled on.

Then there was more trouble. Vargon arrived in a roar of thunder and a wickedly whipping wind storm. Everyone in the chamber was blown off their feet. Timber was flung into the door of the queen's chamber, where the duel was continuing. While Zora's spider venom potion was giving her an edge, Wanda was clearly in trouble. She had a nasty slash on one shoulder, a deep wound on her leg and she was limping. Zora was still walking confidently.

But Timber was in the right place at the right in time. As Zora prepared for a particularly vicious spell, he jumped on her, knocking her to the ground and her wand from her hand. It skidded across the floor and both queens dived for it. Reaching it at the same time, they wrestled on the ground, snatching and grabbing for it as they rolled over. Timber jumped in and pinned Zora down. Wanda got hold of the wand, rolled away and prepared to strike just as Vargon whirled in closer, on his second wind storm. He fired at Timber, throwing him off Zora. He called Zora's wand and it whipped through the air, straight into his hand.

'We're leaving!' he roared, and grabbed Zora by the arm.

But Zora was determined to cast her favourite spell: the Destroyer spell. As Vargon began the shunt to whisk the two of them back to Mord Manor, she snatched her wand from his grip and fired.

'Destructus destras!'

Wanda had guessed Zora's next move, and she hurried to the back wall, unlocked her safe as quickly as she could and took out Cordelia's wand. She twirled around and cast a strong Protection spell just as she heard the dreaded words from Zora's lips. Vargon and Zora disappeared in a red flash as both spells took effect. Timber hobbled over to the queen. He had several burns on one side. Wanda stroked him gently, then stumbled to the floor, as the powerful willow wand suddenly overwhelmed her.

Fortunately for the Wandeleis, Zora had been only partially present when she cast the spell, and Wanda had managed to lessen its force, but the outcome was still very bad. Hollow Hill creaked and rumbled as the entire structure began to crumble. Everyone stopped to listen. The bats and hawks flew quickly out of the tunnels, trying to find the nearest escape route. The animals knew instinctively what was happening, too. Oberon screeched, and Pendrick roared.

'Everyone, out! NOW!'

Dougal had sniffed Timber out and he ran towards the chamber to see if he was all right. Teddy raced after him, followed by Jamie, Pendrick and Thaddeus. The professors assisted the queen, while Jamie and the animals went to Timber.

'Timber's hurt!' cried Jamie. Esther came in with her bottle of tincture. She gave Wanda some first, then looked after Timber and the other animals.

'We'll have to do the rest of the healing later,' said Thaddeus. 'We must leave immediately.' They stayed close together as they hurried towards the tunnel for Grindlewood, but progress was slow. Every tunnel was jammed as everyone tried to outrun the massive cave-in that was starting.

Deep moans and groans filled Hollow Hill as it began to disintegrate. Large cracks appeared all around, overhead and underfoot, like a giant earthquake encircling a crowd. Rubble, dust and smoke thickened, hampering the escape, as chunks of earth collapsed on all sides. It was difficult to breathe, see or move.

Eventually, everyone made it out. The last few witches and wizards were dragged to safety by the dwarfs. They set off in different directions, towards the village, forests and fields. Most of the dwarfs headed for Grindlewood Forest, while Bushfire and Jugjaw followed the children, pets, professors, Wanda and her sisters back to Grindlewood House. As they hurried through the last stretch to the fairy house, they heard tunnel after tunnel collapse behind them.

Chapter Twenty-five

DARKNESS GATHERS

The children escaped with only minor burns and bruises and no poisonous cuts. Ernie used his healing magic on everyone, after Esther and Tamara had first applied plenty of lotion and tincture. Then the residents gathered at the kennel.

'We have to increase our patrols, on the ground and in the air, starting right now,' said Timber, marching up and down in front of his friends.

'We sent word to the starlings,' said Sparky Sparrow. 'We thought you might like them to come.'

'More rabbits are trained up and ready,' said Ramona.

'Three extra pairs of swans have joined us,' said Serena. The pond looked quite elegant with the new swans swimming up and down. Cyril, the grey heron looked impressive, perched on his old lookout post at the top of one of the trees overhanging the pond. It all looked quite normal. No one would suspect they were all on guard.

'Good,' said Timber. 'We're lucky to have so many friends. Zora is bound to return, stronger, more determined and with a better army too.'

'When will this happen?' asked Norville.

'It's impossible to say,' said Timber. 'So far, Zora has only been interested in the queen, but I heard her talk about total revenge. The destruction of Hollow Hill is just a game to her, a way to show off. She has bigger plans, I'm sure of it, and so does Vargon.'

The children sat on the porch of the fairy house and watched the animals and birds. They were all chattering now. Each of them had questions and offered suggestions. Indeed, the whole garden was busy. A small number of witches, wizards and dwarfs had ended up there too. Queen Wanda gave them instructions and they left by the gap in the hedge. Pendrick and Sparks were issuing new DimLocks in the field next door, lockets to take them to the Eastern Woods. Wanda and Esther walked over to the children. Thunder rumbled overhead, but the rain and sleet had stopped.

'Thank you for coming to help us today,' said Wanda. 'You were all extremely brave. I had a feeling something awful might happen, which is why I entrusted you with the keys.'

The children glanced at each other, wondering if this was the right moment to tell the queen that they had found the orb. Luke nudged Jamie a few times, urging him to say something. Abigail's eyes widened, hinting that they shouldn't say a word. It had been a horrid day for the queen, and she had been wounded.

'Um, what are you going to do now?' asked Jamie.

'We will gather and recover in the Eastern Woods,' said Wanda. 'Sebastian Stag has agreed to give us refuge there while Hollow Hill is being rebuilt. The dwarfs are already working through the debris. We haven't enough magic to fix it quickly, but the little we have will help. We might have to consider rebuilding our community somewhere else.'

'Our treasures and scrolls will be locked inside the Great Oak Trees in the Eastern Woods,' said Pendrick, joining them. 'The fairies will remain there too, while they repair *The Book of Darkness*.'

'Zora will take time to recover after using the Destroyer spell,' said Wanda. 'That gives us time to prepare for whatever is coming next.'

'Are we going to the Eastern Woods too?' asked Abigail, turning to her granddad.

'No,' said Thaddeus. 'Your mother and I will remain here until the Grindles get back, then we three will go back to our home in the village.'

'Sparks has set the DimLock to bring you to the Eastern Woods if we need to talk,' said Wanda. 'For now, you should go home, Luke, and all of you should go back to school, back to your normal lives for a while.'

'School? Normal?' cried Jamie. 'In the middle of all this?'

'We can do no more until we restore *The Book of Darkness*,' said Wanda. 'Hopefully it will be ready before Zora recovers and returns with Vargon and whoever else is hiding in Mord Manor.'

'There you all are!' cried Sparks, as he put the DimLock around Abigail's neck. 'Everyone has departed, Your Majesty.'

The queen nodded and looked a little relieved. 'Good luck, children,' she said. 'Timber knows how to keep you safe, and the butterflies will bring a message when we need you. The DimLock has been reset to take you to the Eastern Woods when we send word.'

The queen and three professors stood in the middle of the garden, took out their own lockets and disappeared to the Eastern Woods.

❧

Zora had returned to Mord Manor in triumphant mood, despite feeling dreadfully ill. Vargon was still holding her roughly by the arm when they landed in the hallway. They both slumped on the ground.

'That was fun!' said Zora. 'Even if you had to spoil it at the end.' She wobbled a little as she tried to stand and then smooth her frizzled hair. She snorted at her crumpled, scorched dress. 'I don't think Wanda will be a problem the next time.'

'What nonsense!' roared Vargon, as he struggled off the floor. He grabbed hold of the banisters to steady himself. 'Why couldn't you have waited until we got the orb? Then we could destroy the whole of Grindlewood, including the queen, all of them.'

'Wanda couldn't be foolish enough to keep Othelia's Orb anywhere near her, not in that dump,' said Zora. 'No, it's somewhere else. It has to be. And it's your job to find it, not mine!'

Vargon noticed a meaner look in her eyes, one he had never seen before.

'Now that Hollow Hill has been flattened,' Zora continued, 'the Wandeleis have nowhere to go. They will scatter. They will panic. Then we'll see what kind of a queen little Wanda really is.'

'Indeed we will,' said Vargon. 'And she may surprise you. You really don't need to show off like that. Trust me, the orb will give you everything you desire, if you would just stop acting on a whim!'

'A whim?' she roared back at him. 'Do you expect me to let her rule over *my* realm? They stole that orb from my ancestors, and I will have my revenge, and in a manner of *my* choosing!'

'I may be old, but I'm not stupid!' said Vargon. 'I know *how* to use magic and *when* to use it. AND THIS IS NOT HOW OR WHEN!'

Their arguing continued until they both starting wheezing. They struggled up the staircase to their bedrooms, one at a time, avoiding each other, but still fuming.

While they had been out, Audmund had been busy in the tower. He ignored the angry shouts downstairs and stared instead at the shuddering shape taking solid form before him. The hairs on the back of his neck prickled and he felt his skin crawl. He had taken a terrible risk.

As the shadows gathered and the shape began to look more familiar, Audmund tried to reassure himself. 'I didn't need Vargon's help after all,' he thought. 'I did it all on my own, and now that they're *both* back, things should get very interesting around here.' He trembled as he stepped forward to welcome his new guest, back from Warlock Hell.

The Wandeleis' first few days in the Eastern Woods were unsettling enough, but then the augurers confirmed that Petrifying magic had been used to bring someone back from the dead. They had woken from their trance in a terrible fluster. Shortly after, the butterflies arrived in the garden to give Timber the awful news:

> *Troubles are mounting, evil is growing,*
> *The past has been thrust upon us!*
> *While the palace was falling, the augurer*
> *Audmund*
> *Brought back the warlock Worfeus!*

Then they told the children. Everyone was horrified. Timber insisted on guarding the well himself with all the dogs, cats and foxes close by. The trees were full of the newly arrived starlings, hundreds of birds who were constantly chattering. The garden was literally hopping with rabbits, day and night. The swans and herons flew in and out of the garden in relays. The bees were flying about in swarms, and even the ladybirds were back, keeping watch in their own little way.

Luke and Trigger moved back home and all four children returned to school. The next Saturday, Luke joined the others bright and early in the fairy house. They were looking through their books again.

'All our pets look very busy,' said Jamie, looking out the crooked little window. 'I feel like we should be doing something.'

'We still haven't told anyone about the orb,' said Luke.

'We haven't had the right moment,' said Jamie. 'They're all very busy after what happened to Hollow Hill, and we can't drop in to the Eastern Woods any time we like.'

'We've hardly seen Granddad either,' said Abigail.

'But we'll get a chance to tell him soon.'

'It was great passing all those Easter tests without doing anything,' said Jemima. 'I don't think I'll ever get results that good again.'

'Mum and Dad will be completely amazed with my report card,' said Jamie.

'No updates yet in *The History of Grindlewood*,' said Luke, shutting the book with a loud pop.

'Maybe the bad news goes straight to the witch language part,' said Jemima.

'I don't think Oberon can read that particular language,' said Abigail. The owl had taken a quick look, flew to the windowsill, then stuck his head under his wing.

After a few minutes of silence, Jamie asked a question they had all been worrying about. 'Who do you think is more powerful, Zora or Worfeus?'

'Um, hard to say,' said Luke. 'But won't they hate each other?'

'Probably,' said Abigail. 'But Worfeus might be even worse than before, having been in Warlock Hell.'

'Things are really messed up, aren't they?' said Jemima.

'And it all comes back to Grindlewood's murky past,' said Luke.

'I wonder if we know all the secrets yet,' said Jemima.

'I doubt it,' said Jamie. 'Oh, and Mum and Dad are coming back tomorrow afternoon.'

'At least Mr Peabody kept them out of the way,' said Jemima. 'It's good they missed everything – so far.'

A message to visit the queen arrived the very next morning, much sooner than expected. Using the DimLock, the four children, Timber, Teddy and Oberon arrived at the edge of the beautiful Eastern Woods. Pendrick met them and led them to a clearing that was already turning into a small village. They spotted Ripley in a cage, guarded by a very stout dwarf. Queen Wanda was sitting under a canopy of Jurassic ferns and giant leaves. She gestured to the children to be seated. Timber sat at her feet.

'There will be more battles and more quests,' said the queen. 'We need you to be as prepared as we will be. Unfortunately, we do not know exactly what Worfeus and Zora are planning. Perhaps Vargon has some grand plan, but there is no doubt they will want to destroy us, or at least take back what they believe to be rightfully theirs – Othelia's Orb, once we find it, our magic, this kingdom – but I will not allow it.'

'How are we supposed to deal with Worfeus, Zora, Vargon and all those warlocks and poisonous creatures?' asked Jamie.

'We will train and guide you, Jamie. Each of you will receive special tuition over the coming months, here in the Eastern Woods. You are the *worthy*, and like us, you cannot escape what is coming,' said Wanda. 'We will be prepared. I promise you.' Wanda beckoned two wizards forward. 'These treasures have never been used by children before but you have more than earned them.'

'This is a very special privilege,' added Pendrick, smiling broadly and leading Jamie forward first.

'This is Gorlan's *real* sword and his shield,' said the queen. 'Take them, and use them well.' Pendrick held the sword and shield out for Jamie. He was so surprised he could barely speak. He took them in his hands, admiring them, feeling very proud.

'Thank you, Your Majesty,' he whispered.

'They will give you an extra edge,' said Pendrick.

'You won't need your toy sword any more.'

'And the ring?' said Jamie.

'It will never leave your finger now,' said Wanda. Pendrick gestured to Luke to come forward next. 'Luke, here is another quiver of Hector's arrows, golden arrows, the strongest he ever made. They can penetrate almost anything, and they will always return to you once you use them with Hector's bow.'

Pendrick handed the quiver to Luke.

'Thank you so much, Your Majesty,' he said, touching the gold tips as they glinted in the sunlight.

'Jemima, you have earned the right to learn magic, a great privilege for a non-witch,' said Wanda.

'How did I do that, Your Majesty?'

'It has to do with your brave and generous heart, and your new wand,' said the queen. 'Thaddeus will explain it when you return home. You are to attend spell classes with Abigail from now on. In fact all of you are invited to attend Magical Learning classes – yes, there are ninety-nine books and I know Thaddeus has every one. He will be your instructor on that great subject. Trust me, you will enjoy it!'

'Thank you! I am so thrilled!' said Jemima, beaming from ear to ear.

'Abigail, Pearl has confirmed your place in her Restoration class, and she has asked that you join her to help her work on *The Book of Darkness*. I'm told you are a very talented artist and will learn these skills quickly.'

Abigail nearly swooned. 'Really?' she gasped.

'She'd like you to start tomorrow,' said Wanda. 'After that, she will assist you in repairing *The Book of Enchantments*.'

'That's amazing, thank you, Your Majesty.'

'You must return to Grindlewood now. Thaddeus has a lot to explain, and the Grindles will be home soon. They have a lot to tell you too.' The queen paused for a moment. When she spoke again she looked very serious. 'There is a very grave threat coming. All of us must be very brave and you must never forget that you are the *worthy*. You did not ask to be chosen, but it is still a great privilege that you were. I know you will always make the right choices, even if that means keeping your own secrets.'

The children glanced at each other. Did the queen already know they had found the orb? Perhaps she wanted them to keep it secret a while longer.

'No matter how frightening, troubling or

challenging the quest,' Wanda continued, 'you must look out for one another, bravely fight, believe in good, and in the end you will triumph.' Then she turned to Timber. 'Timber, you are the Guardian of Grindlewood. Protect these children above all else and all will be well.'

Pendrick escorted them back the way they had come. They were quiet on their walk to the edge of the woods. The queen's words were buzzing in their heads. They were comforting and encouraging words, despite the obvious danger that was looming. Sebastian Stag stood watching as they passed. He bowed to them but didn't approach.

'We will send word again when there is news,' said Pendrick.

'Thanks again for all the treasures and the privileges, Professor,' said Jamie.

'You are welcome,' said Pendrick. 'You have earned them.'

Chapter Twenty-six

REVELATIONS

After all the excitement of their visit to the Eastern Woods, the boys put their new treasures carefully away, and they all slumped into bean bags in the fairy house. The last few weeks had been hectic. After a little while, the girls looked at a few spell books to prepare for Jemima's new lessons. Luke took out the *Crypto Riddles* book and started to do more puzzles. He loved the way the book updated with new ones once you finished the whole book.

Jamie began polishing his new sword after he attached his old wooden one to the wall. 'That was a great toy sword,' he said. 'I'm always going to keep it even if I never use it again.'

'Um, I think I just figured something out,' said Luke. 'Something kinda weird.'

'Oh, what?' said Jamie.

The girls looked up from their books.

'There was a funny looking set of symbols on the parchment in Hollow Hill. I couldn't figure it out at the time, so I left it. But I think I've figured it out now.' He read from some notes he had just scribbled: 'Never cross a goblin: stolen gold is neither forgiven nor forgotten.'

'What's that about?' asked Jamie.

'I'm not sure,' said Luke. 'I didn't find anything else like it.'

No one had any idea what it meant. Abigail and Jemima opened a few more books to see if they could find anything about goblins, but they couldn't. Luke returned to his puzzle to make sure he hadn't made a mistake, and Jamie went outside to play with the dogs for a while.

When Thaddeus arrived back from the Eastern Woods, he called everyone into the kitchen. Timber and Teddy came inside to listen.

'Your parents will be back shortly,' said Thaddeus, 'so I must ask you not to say anything about what's been going on here. In fact we need to hear what they have to say. And before that, I have a few things to explain to you.'

'You do? I mean what will Mum and Dad have to say?' asked Jamie.

'Quite a lot, as it happens,' said Thaddeus.

'Herbie Peabody, the solicitor, is a friend of ours,' said Esther. 'He sent his pigeon here with a few messages over the last couple of weeks.'

The children looked from one to the other. This was definitely news. Something was up.

'Mr Peabody was interested in some papers your father found in the cellar,' said Thaddeus. The children nodded; they knew that already. 'Well –'

'Begin at the beginning, Thaddeus,' said Esther. 'They need to know everything.'

'Yes, you're right,' said Thaddeus. 'The story begins with your great-great-uncle George and his young and foolish sister, Gemima.'

'Oh!' said Jemima.

'Spelled with a *G*,' said Thaddeus. 'Gemima loved magic, just as you do, dear, but one day someone came to her with an offer she couldn't refuse.'

'What was that?' asked Abigail.

'A goblin offered Gemima the "gift" of magic in exchange for gold. George was a wealthy man and he owned quite a lot of gold. Gemima knew this of course and did the deal with the goblin, but without telling her brother, and that's really when all the trouble started.'

'A goblin,' muttered Luke.

'Yes, unsavoury characters, most of them,' said Thaddeus. 'Turns out the goblin's enchantment didn't last long and Gemima died within the year.'

'That's terrible!' said Jemima.

'Not only that, but the gold she paid the goblin turned out to be *goblin* gold bars, and then George got into a lot of trouble.'

'What happened him?' asked Jamie. 'Where did he get goblin gold?'

'Mr Peabody is looking into that,' said Thaddeus. 'George Grindle only died about ten years ago, at a very great age, outliving even his nieces and nephews, which means he managed to keep the goblins at bay somehow, but then ...'

'What?' asked all four children.

'The goblins left Grindlewood to fight over a huge discovery of gold in another dimension,' said Esther. 'No one was sorry to see them go.'

'The important point is this,' said Thaddeus. 'George's sister Gemima was Greg's great-aunt, so we think this is how you can do magic, Jemima – you are a blood relation, and although it skipped two generations, we believe that a little bit of her magic might have passed to you.'

Jemima gasped so deeply she almost fainted.

'That is so cool!' cried Jamie. 'Wait a minute, the magic killed our great-great um, great-grand-auntie. Will that kill Jemima too?'

'No,' said Thaddeus. 'Jemima's magic was inherited.'

'Is that how Gorlan's ring works for Jamie?' asked Jemima.

'That could be part of it,' said Thaddeus.

'What about the wand?' asked Abigail. 'Where did it come from?'

'The wand is fine,' said Thaddeus. 'There is no trace of malice, but its origins are still a mystery. I've asked Flint to look into it further.'

'You mentioned goblins,' said Luke. 'I found something about goblin gold in the *Crypto Riddles* book just now.'

'Oh? Tell me,' said Thaddeus.

Luke explained.

'You could be right,' said Thaddeus. 'Show me

that puzzle later, and I'll see if I come up with the same answer.'

'How was George so wealthy?' asked Jamie.

'He had a number of different businesses,' said Thaddeus, 'and he made quite a fortune, but sadly, we think he may have hoodwinked the goblins out of some gold too, and they don't like being fooled. But that wand is now rightfully yours, Jemima. It chose you and you may keep it.'

'It's no wonder we have to fix all these troubles,' said Jamie. 'Our ancestors were involved in dodgy stuff.'

'Like I said, Mr Peabody is still looking into all that,' said Thaddeus. 'We'll soon find out how much he told your parents, hopefully nothing too difficult to explain.'

The front door opened. Greg and Gloria were home. Suddenly, there was great excitement in the house.

'Well, that's the biggest welcome ever,' said Gloria, giving the children big hugs.

'After the longest short trip ever,' said Greg. 'And do we have news for you?'

The children stared at their parents. They had news

too, but they couldn't say anything.

'How about some soothing hot chocolate?' said Esther. 'Supper won't be ready for another hour.' Thaddeus smiled broadly at the Grindles, allowing his gold tooth to sparkle. Everyone gathered around the kitchen table. Timber and Teddy stayed inside to hear everything. The rest of the animals were on duty.

'He was quite a character, my great-uncle George,' said Greg. 'Apparently, he was a good businessman, made some money, lost it, made it again, and then the trail stopped. No one is quite sure how or when he made enough money to build this huge house and garden. He was a keen writer, too, and kept notes on everything. I want to check around the house and see if I can find any more papers or diaries, and I might even knock that old wall, the one that closes off the far end of the cellar.'

'You never know what secrets might be lurking in a cellar!' said Gloria.

'I'm determined to find out everything about him,' said Greg. 'He's such an intriguing character. I wish I'd met him a long time ago. Isn't it exciting to know we have such interesting ancestors?'

No one knew what to say to that.

It was time for Timber and Teddy's patrol. Jamie let them out and they trotted around the garden with Eldric. Oberon and four swans flew overhead.

'What do you think about this George guy?' asked Teddy. 'Does it really matter what he got up to? It all happened so long ago.'

'We'll have to undo any trouble he caused,' said Timber.

'I wonder how many people he upset,' said Eldric.

'And how many were magical people,' said Teddy.

'I've a feeling we're going to hear more about that,' said Timber.

'But first there's Zora and her gang,' tooted Oberon, just above them.

'I've been trying to work out what Audmund's up to,' said Timber. 'Let's hope he didn't have the keys copied for Worfeus. If he did, he might go looking for the orb – and he might find it. The first lock was in his lair.'

'Seems to me that all of them are up to something,' said Teddy. 'Question is: have they all got the same plan or different plans?'

'I was wondering about that too,' said Timber. 'But maybe that's to our advantage.'

Later that night, Timber howled for a very long time. There were so many dangers, so many unanswered questions, yet there was nothing they could do to stop any of it happening. It was like watching a storm gather and head right towards you.

Back in Mord Manor, Bodric had returned. He was eager to find Zora, preferably alone. He felt sure she would like to know what the eagle was up to, and the Grindlewood Army too. He had been startled, however, to discover that he could no longer call her with his thoughts. 'Perhaps the Mind-meld is broken, or maybe she's saving her strength,' he thought, trying to convince himself that he wasn't about to be banished. He fluttered into the parlour where Vargon, Audmund and a trembling Phineas were waiting for Zora. Audmund had been looking for Phineas when he accidently arrived in Grindlewood garden.

'Oh, there you are,' said Audmund. 'I thought you'd run away.'

'I'm back. I mean, no,' said Bodric, nervously. It

took him a moment to realise who the shadowy figure standing at the window was. He nearly choked.

'Who is so important that my beauty treatment must be disturbed?' said Zora as she swept into the parlour. She turned immediately to Vargon. Then she heard a voice she could never forget.

'I must say, I like the new image. *Extra* red, is it? Very fetching.'

Zora whirled around. 'Who – brought – you – back?' she snarled.

'Steady on, sister dear, we're on the same side now, and I've learned a trick or two in Warlock Hell, so you might want to be nice to me.' He stood there grinning at her, bold as brass. 'Vargon tells me we're going after Othelia's Orb. Sounds like a devilish plan. Now, tell me, what else have I missed?'

Worfeus was back.

THE END

Acknowledgements

A huge thank you once again to all the 'super-team' – Robert Doran (editor), Chenile Keogh and Vanessa O'Loughlin (Kazoo), Fintan Taite (illustrator), Andrew Brown and Nigel Baker (graphic design), all the bookstores and libraries that continue to support my work, and every enthusiastic young reader who enjoys the magic of Grindlewood.

A special mention also for my friend Peri, who introduced me to the beautiful Timber, and as always a heartfelt thank you to my biggest fan, supporter, advisor and confidant, my husband Angelo.

Book 1

THE SECRETS OF GRINDLEWOOD

Jamie and Jemima Grindle move to Grindlewood House with their pets Timber and Teddy. But they soon realise that all is not as it seems in their beautiful new garden. There is dark magic at work in the nearby forest.

The good witch Wanda has been defeated and now the wicked warlock Worfeus is plotting to destroy Grindlewood and its enchanted garden. Only Wanda's powerful spells, written on a secret scroll, can rid the world of the warlock.

Timber must lead the animals of Grindlewood in their quest to find the scroll and defeat their enemy. But where is the scroll hidden and will they find it before Worfeus? Is there really enough magic in their wild garden to help them defeat such evil?

Book 2

THE SECRET SCROLL

Grindlewood Book 2: The Secret Scroll follows the animals of Grindlewood garden as they continue the quest to save their enchanted home. The odds are stacked against them as they struggle to understand the ancient language of Wanda's secret scroll and use its magic to defeat the evil Worfeus.

Slowly Jamie and Jemima learn that their pets are caught up in something both sinister and special and that somehow they must find a way to help. All the while, the wicked warlock is growing more powerful and threatening.

The race is on to unlock the secrets of the scroll before Worfeus frees himself from the forest and enters the garden himself, intent on revenge and the destruction of Grindlewood.

Book 3

THE QUEEN'S QUEST

When she hears that the residents of Grindlewood garden have defeated the wicked warlock Worfeus, the Forest Queen decides to enlist their help to release her from the Worfagon's curse. But it soon becomes clear that the Queen is not the kind and gentle leader she once was.

After years of suffering under the Worfagon 'tree spell', the Queen is now bitter and angry. She is obsessed with Jamie's beautiful dog, Timber, and she threatens to keep him for herself unless the children agree to come to her aid. They must find the lost *Ancient Book of Magic*, which holds powerful spells that can free her.

Timber the brave malamute dog once again leads Jamie, Jemima and their loyal band of pets in a hair-raising adventure. Together they must face down mortal danger, dark magic and evil enemies to free the trapped Forest Queen and ensure Timber's safe return.

Book 3

INDEPENDENCE